Warsaw Tales

Warsaw
Tales

Stories selected and
translated by
Antonia Lloyd-Jones

Edited by
Helen Constantine

OXFORD
UNIVERSITY PRESS

OXFORD
UNIVERSITY PRESS

Great Clarendon Street, Oxford, OX2 6DP,
United Kingdom

Oxford University Press is a department of the University of Oxford.
It furthers the University's objective of excellence in research, scholarship,
and education by publishing worldwide. Oxford is a registered trade mark of
Oxford University Press in the UK and in certain other countries

Published in the United States of America by Oxford University Press
198 Madison Avenue, New York, NY 10016, United States of America

British Library Cataloguing in Publication Data
Data available

Library of Congress Control Number: 2024906506

ISBN 978-0-19-285556-5

Printed and bound by CPI Group (UK) Ltd,
Croydon, CR0 4YY

Contents

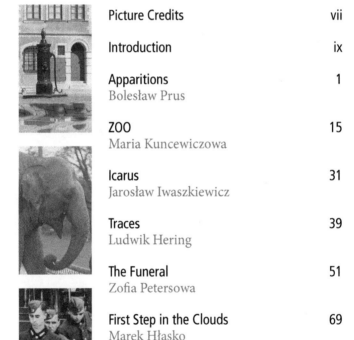

Picture Credits

Introduction

Warsaw is Europe's phoenix: almost eighty years since its destruction in 1944 it is still rising from the ashes, spreading its wings with ever more vitality.

The accidental irony of the city's English-language name could not be more cruel, as few cities have 'seen war' on a similar scale. But long before the Nazis razed it to the ground, Warsaw had already had a particularly thorny history, suffering turbulent events including the Swedish invasion of the mid-seventeenth century and the power struggles surrounding the eighteenth-century partitions of Poland.

For most of the nineteenth century Poland was wiped off the map by the neighbouring powers, and Warsaw became the third largest city in the Russian Empire, as well as a hotbed of revolt, the starting point for the three major uprisings of 1794, 1830, and 1863. After the First World War Poland regained independence, and in 1920 Warsaw was successfully defended against the Red Army's aggressive attempts to export the Russian Revolution. During the

Second World War, Warsaw was at the epicentre of violence and tragedy, not only the site of the largest Jewish ghetto, but also of the bravest urban resistance, epitomized by the heroic but doomed Warsaw Uprising. The Nazis then blew the city up as they fled the advancing Soviets—who lingered on the eastern side of the river Vistula to let the Germans destroy the heart of Poland.

But after the war Warsaw showed how irrepressible it is—its motto is *Semper invicta*, meaning 'Always invincible'—and it can boast some of the world's most spectacular reconstruction of historical buildings, a process that still continues. Since Poland became a free, democratic country again in 1989, the city has had a new burst of strength, and nowadays it feels like an energetic modern capital. Although on my first visit, in the 1980s, the impression I had was of a wounded city, today it feels vibrant, buzzing with cultural events, sporting new buildings and exciting architectural projects. It's as if something I'd been seeing in black and white had burst into colour—just like in the final story in this collection.

The city's Polish name is Warszawa, which folklore explains as a combination of the names Wars and Sawa, mythological city-founding figures who in one version of the legend were siblings, in another a married couple; however, in my favourite version Sawa was a mermaid living in the river Vistula, with whom a fisherman named

Wars fell in love. Beyond her appearances in various myths, the mermaid took up permanent residence on the city's coat of arms, as its patron and defender, with her sword raised to fight off invaders. Visitors will see her immortalized in a number of monuments (as on the cover of this book), and on the doors of the city's officially approved taxis.

These founding myths are also among the first short stories associated with Warsaw, a city with a strong literary tradition. The legends associated with Warsaw are so enduring that some new versions were written as recently as 2016, for a beautifully illustrated anthology published by the Museum of Warsaw, which gathers renderings of these stories dating from the nineteenth century through to the modern day. Visitors will find a selection of them published in English at the museum, in the Old Town Marketplace.

The Old Town Marketplace—largely reconstructed in the 1950s—is the first port of call for most of Warsaw's tourists, and I too chose it as the starting point for this literary tour of the city. I should explain the criteria for my rather eclectic, and of course personal choice of stories for this book, which I hope will provide an introduction to a possibly unfamiliar city. With this aim in mind, I adopted some principles that have influenced my selection: I wanted to tell some of the city's history through the stories (in historical terms, they are more or less in chronological order); to include a number of authors who have not previously appeared in English translation; to include not just fiction but also some literary nonfiction, which is a strong genre in Polish literature; and finally to feature identifiable locations all over Warsaw, in the hope that this set of stories can act as a form of guidebook to the city, for the reader who likes to explore.

I also wanted to convey the sense of a dialogue between the present and the past that the visitor to Warsaw inevitably feels. My first story, 'Apparitions', written in 1911, refers to Warsaw's past history: times of both opulence and indigence. Just over a century later, more recent history is inescapable in Warsaw. As in every major city, there are the usual monuments and statues commemorating great historical figures, such as Nicolaus Copernicus, or King Zygmunt III, but not many capital cities can boast a seventeenth-century royal castle made of reinforced concrete. Every few steps you take in the city centre, and quite far beyond it, you will see a plaque or a carved stone memorializing victims of the Nazi occupation who died on that spot. They are so frequent that I am afraid of ceasing to notice them, but I recommend lingering occasionally to decipher the Polish message, and to reflect. (One of these, in the northern suburb of Żoliborz, appears in the story 'The View from Above and Below', which takes us back to the late 1920s and then to the same location in the 1990s.) In Muranów, the district where the Jewish ghetto was located during the war, you will find a sobering trail of remembrance from the Ghetto Uprising Monument— sculpted from a slab of labradorite Hitler shipped to Poland for his own victory monument—past the bunker where the last brave fighters died during the Ghetto Uprising, and on to the Umschlagplatz, where another monument commemorates all those who were herded onto trains here for their final journey to the death camps. Two of the stories in this collection remember the ghetto: 'Traces' is about the children who went in and out of it in an effort to find food, and 'The Presence' is about the ghosts that still haunt the area.

Yet despite the tragic echoes, today's Warsaw is very much alive, and as you walk south from the Royal Castle down the elegant sweep of Krakowskie Przedmieście, it will be hard to imagine that this is where the wartime scene described in 'Icarus' took place, or that as recently as in 1981 the university gates were festooned in strike banners and crowds of anti-government protestors—as described in the story 'Che Guevara'. Though the city's fighting spirit persists to this day. Looking west from here, you won't be able to miss the sight of the sky-scraping, 237-metre Palace of Culture and Science, Stalin's gift in 1955 to the Polish nation, that never lets anyone forget that for forty-five years this country was a Soviet satellite, under the gaze of Big Brother; protests continue to be held beneath this—to some still sinister—edifice. Its two-faced nature is described here in 'The Palace of Culture', though these days its dominance is muted by the cluster of more modern glass towers that surround it. Of these, only the EU's highest building, the 310-metre Varso Tower office block, completed in 2022, is taller.

Continue south down Nowy Świat Street, where the title character from 'Che Guevara' sits in a café, and you will come to Three Crosses Square, where the hero of 'Return of the Evil One' is caught in a time warp that returns him to the 1950s—or rather to a literary version of it.

Warsaw has a very good transport system, but throughout the 1980s the metro was nothing more than a string of fenced-off excavations with twisted metal protruding from them. My favourite transport is the bikes to be hired on many street corners; anyone inspired to explore the river Vistula, featured here in 'The Warsaw Map', might wish to take a pleasant bike ride north from the centre along the river embankment, all the way to the leafy suburb of Żoliborz (the location for 'A View from Above and Below'). Here and in nearby Marymont there are still allotment gardens like those described in 'First Step in the Clouds', an enduring feature of the city.

In between the southern end of Żoliborz and the north of Muranów lies one of Warsaw's most historic sites, Powązki Cemetery, a huge, atmospheric necropolis where traditionally the great and the good are buried. It appears here in 'The Funeral', where a burial takes place of a kind that was frequent during the war. This story also depicts the devastation of the city that followed the failed Warsaw Uprising, as well as the indomitable spirit of the citizens who set about clearing the rubble.

Crossing the river, as in the story 'ZOO', takes you to the Praga district, the modernized zoo, and the riverside beaches, which are still more or less the same as in the 1930s. South from Praga is the attractive Saska Kępa district, home to the eponymous hero of 'Che Guevara', and now to some excellent restaurants.

Warsaw makes frequent appearances in Polish literature and is the setting not just for numerous short stories but many novels. Inevitably, for lack of space there are stories that, to my regret, I have failed to include here by authors strongly associated with Warsaw. In my 'Notes on the Authors and Stories, with Suggestions for Further Reading', I try to point the reader towards some of the novels available in English translation that are set in Warsaw and where the city has an integral role, like one of the characters itself.

My thanks are due to the many people who made suggestions for this collection, including Mariusz Szczygieł (who lent me a book of stories by the virtually unknown Zofia Petersowa and who inspired Hanna Krall to write the true story described in 'The Presence'); Timothy Snyder for introducing me to the work of Ludwik Hering; Jacek Dehnel for lending me a collection that was the source of Krzysztof Varga's story; Magda Heydel for her help with Maria Kuncewiczowa's difficult prose; and Sean Bye for giving me the book of Kuncewiczowa's essays that contains 'ZOO'. Thank you also to Darek Fedor for lending me a flat in Powiśle, Warsaw, where I was able to do much of the research for this book at the Warsaw University library. I am hugely grateful to all the copyright owners and their agents who have so generously given their permission for these stories to be published in this book—many thanks to you all. And a big thank-you to everyone at OUP, including Emma Varley, Emma Slaughter, picture researcher Deborah Protheroe, and my extremely patient series editor, Helen Constantine, for all their support. Finally, I'd like to say thank you to all the friends who make Warsaw one of my favourite places to be.

Antonia Lloyd-Jones

Apparitions
(1911)

Bolesław Prus

Here we have an accurate account by the Lithuanian gentleman Heavsiło of a strange incident that befell him in Warsaw. We would be disinclined to believe this tale, if it hadn't been confirmed by two reliable witnesses.

'I arrived in Warsaw,' says Heavsiło, 'not exactly with ready cash, but with money orders for a few thousand, wishing to acquire an inexpensive apartment here in your city, for perhaps one hundred and fifty, perhaps two hundred thousand roubles; poor fellow that I am, I can't afford more than that. But as in Wilno I'd heard a lot about your thieves and swindlers, instead of putting up at an inn, I tracked down an old friend, Posteksilski, from my time in Siberia, and lodged with him on Podwale Street.

'Hardly have I settled in, and hardly have my friend and I set foot outside, when at once we are accosted by a fine fellow of middling years, with a rosy nose and a smooth tongue—an acquaintance of Posteksilski's by name of Sotkiewicz; having quizzed me on the spot as to the purpose of my visit, he advises us to go to the Old Town.

'"Not because Fukier's wineshop is on the Marketplace, God forbid!" says the fine fellow, "but perhaps our dear Lithuanian friend will spot a house for himself up that way, which he will buy and renovate. To his own credit, and to the benefit of the entire nation."

'"Aha!" think I, "if the entire nation without exception is to benefit from it, then perhaps I should buy a house on the Marketplace…"

'We pass a few small streets, until Sotkiewicz speaks up again: "Oh, here's Fukier's place, but I shan't insist on entering, as times are hard…And here's our beloved Old Town Marketplace."

'I look around…Well, houses like any others. Just one thing doesn't much appeal to me—the square is crammed full of stalls, with crowds of Jews at them, on the pavements and in the entrance halls, and there's a palpable stench…No decent man would want to rent rooms in such a place…

'Hardly have I said it, when Sotkiewicz cries out: "How can there not be Jews if Christians won't buy the houses? If every rich Lithuanian bought just one house on the Marketplace and maintained it properly, you wouldn't find a stench here even if you paid for it."

' "You people were quite able to burn Warsaw down," he goes on shouting, "but when it comes to atonement, when it comes to compensation for your sins you're not here!"

' "For the love of God, sir," say I, "who did you say burned Warsaw down?"

' "The Lithuanians," the fellow replies, "in the year 1669 ... I shall never forgive them to the day I die."

' "Zounds!" think I. But I'm not well versed in history, so instead of arguing, I reply: "So what sort of a fellow is this Fukier? He sells wine, it seems? Perhaps it would do to drop in on him for a thimbleful?"

' "You must be joking!" interjects my friend from Siberia. "Who drinks wine these days? Times have changed ... "

'But the fine fellow who latched onto us in Podwale Street cries out again: "Why not drink wine? What's the merchant to do with it—pour it into the gutter? As the Lithuanians were pleased to burn Warsaw down, let them now at least quench the thirst of the descendants of the unfortunate citizens whose homes were reduced to ashes ... "

'Merciful God! On my life, I never imagined I was born of arsonists! Oh well, if the man regards himself as an injured party, too bad—let him determine the penalty.

'So despite the resistance of my Siberian friend, we enter the wineshop.

'"At the very least," says the worried Posteksilski, "don't have expensive wine…The Crimean here shouldn't be too bad…"

'"Crimean? At Fukier's?" roars Sotkiewicz. "Do you know what I rinse with Crimean wine? Certainly not my throat!"

'"A light Sauterne, then," whispers my friend, who has been told to avoid strong drink because of hardened arteries.

'But Sotkiewicz isn't even listening. He goes up to the waiter and starts giving orders in an undertone: "Bring us a small bottle of my usual, the one I always start with…Then a bottle of the one I usually drink after that…Then we'll see, but at the very end bring us a bottle of the one I always finish with, if I'm in the company of good patriots."

'"Well," I'm thinking, "Warsaw is an unfortunate city, but people know how to console themselves here too. Indeed, one would find the same types in Wilno as well— we have suffered too, oh yes, we've suffered a great deal…"

'Sotkiewicz leads us into a dark, separate little room, seats us at a table, and when the waiter brings the bottle, he sets about filling the glasses himself.

'I tell you, my goodness, when I taste the wine that comes first, it gives me a sense of bliss; and when I drink the one that comes second, I feel the desire to sing. And what do you think, I sing so wonderfully, so soulfully that tears well up in my eyes. Then it occurs to me: "Merciful God! A man must travel all the way to Warsaw to find out he's a singer."

'Then I look, and I see I'm not the only one who's weeping. Sotkiewicz has tears the size of peas flowing down his cheeks, and my Siberian friend, Posteksilski, is resting his head on his hand and just quivering.

'"The Jews will eat us up," says Posteksilski, "they'll eat us up, as sure as eggs is eggs. They'll eat us up, vomit us into the Vistula, and off we'll float to Danzig..."

'"Violeński...my brother Pole, don't talk like that!" Sotkiewicz interrupts him.

'"But I'm not Violeński, I'm Posteksilski..."

'"It's all the same—you don't have to argue over a stupid name...And the Jews aren't going to eat us up. Just as that bushy isle in the middle of the Vistula goes under water every year and then rises to the surface again, so our Old Town has more than once sunk in disaster but has always floated to the top...Lumbagski..."

'"But I'm not Lumbagski, I'm Posteksilski."

'"It's all the same. But you're my brother...a Pole...So give us a kiss and let the beast of a Lithuanian pay, since he burned Warsaw down..."

'Only at this moment, I tell you, goodness me, do I remember that there's just one Lithuanian among us. "Which one could it be?", I start to think. Then I look round, and … on the dark wall of the room I notice a small, bright circle, which slowly grows larger; at its centre something is moving, like variegated grubs, and it's murmuring too. So I ask my companions, my Siberian friend and Sotkiewicz: "Can you see what's happening on the wall?" And my friend says: "Yes, we can." While Sotkiewicz adds: "It must be a cinematograph! And I swear blind it's showing us something that looks like our beloved Old Town … I can even hear voices … "

'"It must be a talking cinematograph…" says Posteksilski.

'Whether my companions have said something else, I do not know, because I am entirely engrossed in what I'm seeing and hearing. And here is our extraordinary vision:

'Summer, daybreak. The Old Town Marketplace, naturally. In the middle of the square, not particularly well cobbled, rises a now non-existent town hall. Around it two rows of houses can be seen: one forms part of the northern, the other part of the western side of the Marketplace. Houses with thick stone walls, painted in colours: red, green, blue, and decorated with images of saints, lions, gryphons, and warships. Some of the images and cornices are gilded; the doors are of iron, the windows solidly barred.

'Several wagons drive out of a side street—they're as big as cottages, harnessed to four and to six horses; the waggoners have heavy sabres at their sides. The wagons stop, male servants run out of the gateways and unload their cargo. There are crates full of velvet, cloth, silk and linen fabrics. There are barrels of wine and sacks of spices from warm countries. There's glass, clocks, weapons and bars of iron. They carry all these goods and many, many others into storerooms and cellars, where the servants arrange them and the shop clerks make records.

'Outside it's becoming ever lighter; the Marketplace disappears, and instead of it we can see a merchant's residence. Enormous wardrobes and four-poster beds, heavy tables and carved chairs, sideboards of the same kind. There are Chinese porcelain and ivory trinkets on the side tables, and silver platters and golden goblets on the dressers. The lady of the house walks across the room; over a sky-blue silk robe she has a second gown, open at the front, and with a long train behind. On her head there's a velvet hood embroidered with gold, in her ears there are diamonds, around her neck pearls, and in her hands a prayer book fastened with golden clasps. This is the merchant's wife. A wondrous beauty, she's going to the chapel for morning Mass, at the hour when the royal court is there.

'Meanwhile, the merchant, in a black velvet doublet and tight breeches, takes a key from the bag at his belt and opens an iron door in the wall. There stand two quarter-bushel pots full of silver thalers and some three-gallon kegs filled with gold. He calls one of his helpers and scatters a few handfuls of coins into his apron to pay the waggoners for the goods they've brought.

'Roughly the same scene is repeated in all the houses on the Marketplace. Everywhere there are refined furnishings, rich carpets, women ornate in silks and expensive gems, proud merchants, and kegs full of gold and silver behind iron doors. Opulence pours through the gates and windows.

'After Mass, the Marketplace fills. Noblemen and noblewomen, street traders, knights in tall boots with jingling spurs, monks, lay clergymen, craftsmen, townsmen, townswomen, beggars, all heading for the stores, some to go shopping, others to earn a living or for alms.

'"This would seem to be the early seventeenth century…Warsaw was beautiful in those days, what?" sobbed Sotkiewicz, wiping his tears with one hand, while raising the glass to his lips with the other.

'The image fades, and shortly after another one emerges. It's the same city, but there's disquiet in the Marketplace. The crowd is running to the north side, and we can hear the hurried ringing of bells. Soon, clouds of thick, black smoke and bright flames appear above the houses, filling the entire scene.

' "That's the fire the Lithuanians caused!" whispers Sotkiewicz.

' "Can't you give it a rest!" Posteksilski scolds him angrily.

'And I, my goodness, I do nothing... I just look, listen, and gush with tears. It's no longer my wonderful singing that's governing my mood, but memories... What can that have been? Where on earth is it?

'The blood-red background of the picture starts to grow clearer. Gradually the smoke settles, and instead of the luxurious houses we can see windows with no glass, blackened walls and protruding chimneys; inside the apartments there are heaps of stones and scorched timber.

' "At that time it was worse in Warsaw than today!" whispers Sotkiewicz.

' "If that's how you want to see it...," replies Posteksilski. "Better under your own smouldering ruins than under a foreign boot..."

' "Sacred words!" I want to say. But it crosses my mind that it might be a dangerous thing to say, so I bite my tongue.

'A new image appears. The Marketplace, but with no trace of the fire in it. White houses, in the windows rugs, flowers, and well-dressed women, in the streets the crowd is kneeling with heads bared. We can hear the sound of bells and cannon fire, guild flags flutter in the wind, and there's music and church singing from somewhere nearby. There's a multitude of people, their clothes are clean and even rich, their faces cheerful. There's a thanksgiving ceremony in progress, maybe to celebrate a victory? In any case, neither the buildings nor the faces show any trace of the past defeat.

'"You see how Warsaw rose again from the conflagration?" shouts Sotkiewicz.

'Once more our room becomes dark; the image vanishes, and moments later something entirely different appears. The Marketplace is almost empty, the iron doors of the houses are locked, the windows are boarded shut. In front of the town hall, several soldiers won't let anyone approach, but threaten to shoot. Some people dressed in red, with crosses on their chests, are carrying stretchers covered with black cloth, at the sight of which the rare passers-by genuflect, and then quickly run away.

'At a turn in the street an affluently dressed man falls with a shout. From around the corner of a building a ragamuffin darts out, scans the scene, and begins to search the fallen man's pockets. Just then the guards arrive. At the sound of a horn, the people dressed in red run up and take away the recumbent man; meanwhile the guards seize the ragamuffin by the arms, lead him to two pillars joined at the top by a beam, and hang him from it.

'"I know! I know!" exclaims Sotkiewicz. "That's the plague in Warsaw."

'Meanwhile, in the image the people have gradually disappeared; a few corpses are left in the Marketplace, and a Dominican praying over them.

' "I know! I know!" repeats Sotkiewicz. "That was when almost everyone in the city died. It was worse than today!"

' "Who knows what's worse," muttered my friend the Siberian, "to die, or to become a ne'er-do-well?"

'Meanwhile, a new image has slowly loomed out of the darkness. The same Old Town Marketplace, but full of people, good cheer and joyful shouts. The houses are new and sumptuous, with rugs and pennants in some of the windows. A procession is moving towards the church, a wedding one of course: the bridegroom is on horseback, in a violet silk tail coat, his best men are in colourful foreign attire or noblemen's robes, decked in white, the bride and her bridesmaids are in litters, and behind them come several ornate carriages with older ladies inside them. We hear pistol shots, shouts from the crowd, and music. In front of the town hall, two oxen are being roasted, and nearby there's a mountain of loaves and a dozen or more barrels of beer for the common folk. Gazing at those bright, lavish houses, and at all those people, well fed, laughing and singing, a man could never imagine he was looking at the same city where so recently plague and pestilence were raging!

' "Dammit," cries Sotkiewicz, "didn't I say our beloved Warsaw would scramble out of that mess too? Like the island in the Vistula: whenever the water floods it, it rises back to the surface."

'"Until the day it drowns lock, stock and barrel…" adds Posteksilski.

'"You're drunk, Bum…Bumblewicz?"

'"My name is not Bumblewicz!" replies my Siberian friend with ire.

'Meanwhile, two more images pass before us. In one we can see today's Old Town with its stalls, its Jews, and its slovenliness. It looks as if the mud never dries on the pavements, and the walls of the houses aren't made of bricks, but of dirt.

'"Here are the results of our negligence!" screams Sotkiewicz. "You people are rascals, and that's that!"

'"Try to speak in the singular," Posteksilski reprimands him.

'The final image is a simply wonderful phenomenon. Rather than the Old Town, it must be a fantastical metropolis! Houses of all possible hues, but light and subtle ones, covered in murals and bas-reliefs, like priceless caskets. And the subject of the murals is the history of each house and its owners over several hundred years! Instead of ordinary stones, the Marketplace is paved in multicoloured mosaics; at its centre there's a lovely little garden, ablaze with real flowers. The place is full of children, schoolboys, elegant women, and foreigners, who have come merely to tour our marvel and pay tribute to its beauties and curiosities. For some of the houses on the Marketplace have become museums housing collections from all over the country.

'"Look, you see, our Warsaw has climbed to the top again!" says Sotkiewicz.

'The image vanishes, and the waiter appears in our little room. We glance at our watches—it is late by now! I pay the bill, which isn't in fact large, for such extraordinary things.

'"What a fine cinematograph you have here!" says Posteksilski.

'"I'm sorry, sir, what cinematograph?" asks the waiter in amazement.

'"The one that shows the Old Town…"

'"I'm sorry, but that can't be here at Fukier's…"

'"How do you explain that?" interrupts Sotkiewicz, forcibly escorting my Siberian friend outside.

'Once we have crossed the threshold, I hear the waiter say to another: "I've chanced upon various tipplers in my time: some that have seen devils, snakes, and vermin… But never before have I met a drunk who saw a cinematograph in an empty room."

'"He's talking about us!" says Sotkiewicz, outraged. He wants to go back into the wineshop to raise a row, but—he can't find the door handle, and by the time he finally does, he's forgotten what it was all about.

'And so we wander sadly home.'

ZOO (1938)

Maria Kuncewiczowa

On Krakowskie I hail a droshky and tell the driver to take me to the Zoological Garden. The vehicle is extremely nippy, not like any other droshky. The driver spent some time working on the speeding horse before it yielded to persuasion, turned around and went in the right direction. The cabbie is seething with energy too—he's one of those low-key Don Juans that are typical along the Vistula, bandit and jester rolled into one. He grabs hold of the reins and goes full speed ahead towards the Staszic Palace.

'Where are we going, when the Zoological Garden is across the river, in the Praga district?' I protest.

He cracks the whip and disagrees: 'I'm going as needs must, up the Avenue.'

'Why take the Avenue?' I say in despair, 'when the garden is in Praga, beyond the Lunapark.'

He stops the horse, turns around on the box and thunders from on high: 'Then you should have said the Lunapark. But to the *Bertonical* Garden you needs must go up the Avenue.'

I pass no further comment on the misunderstanding and we're on our way to Praga. It's a Sunday in June, the sun is shining and the streets are full of people. The driver has a bushy moustache, small, impish eyes and a keen, twitching hooter of a nose. In the same belligerent tone in which he has just been arguing about where we're going, now he starts praising his horse.

'He's wiser than an artiste,' he says, 'there's five of 'em at the stable, and he'll eat their leavings too. You saw how he tore away when we was driving fer nothing? And now he's put his head down! He's not so dumb as to rip off when he felt a passenger.'

There are taxis bowling along the bridge in a tight pack, and the driver curses.

'What the devil, the traffic, the crush in this city, you've gotta keep up with the machines, you've gotta keep up with life—and you can't use the bloody whip here, or he'll turn the whole droshky over.' He's looking at the horse's rump with lust and regret. Then the bridge ends, and we drive a short stretch downhill. Only now does the driver loosen his whip and lash the horse again and again. He's laughing from deep inside, and the horse is shuddering with pain, but it's running very smoothly. I no longer have any idea which of them is wiser than an artiste—the super-humanly patient horse, or the bestial driver.

'Why are you doing that?' I ask.

' 'Cos if the droshky's pushing him down the hill, he can't do nothing, and you can teach him a lesson.'

And he 'teaches him' some more, inflating his Don Juan-ish, rooster-like but fleshy, misshapen nose.

In a clump of greenery on the Praga riverbank, turned to face Warsaw, three enormous letters come into sight: ZOO. When this grand abbreviation catches the eye, a thrilling European shiver runs down the Varsovian spine. The ZOO is a bourgeois luxury, it's culture on a Sunday, it's caring about our brother-wolves and our sister-leopards, it's kiddywinks wriggling on the backs of good-natured exotic creatures, and above all it's an illusion of Berlin, of a capital steeped in the best beer, and starlit by the most fabulous electrics. Hidden in the bushes on the Vistula, the ZOO intrigues and stirs ambitious hopes.

We push our way across the Praga public park, amid clusters of soldiers out romancing on a pass, amid people in floor-length satin dresses, berets and tennis shoes. Thick dust fills our throats, the prams give off a stench of rarely bathed infants, older children alternately munch and roll along bread rings given them by unfamiliar uncles. If someone snatches this treat off them, they scurry to complain to aunts, sisters or mothers, and the uncles in uniforms ask from a distance: 'Get lost or I'll give you a hiding'—then retreat with the women into the unseemly elderberry groves.

There's a queue at the gates of the zoo: it's a school outing. Suntanned lads, and lasses all but set solid with thick, provincial cream. Altogether full of festivity and trouble. Not a trace of the saucy nonchalance that reduces and lightens the wait for the big-city paupers. At the head of the outing there's a model teacher couple: she represents energy and motherliness, while he's the epitome of moral leadership. So she is soliciting for discounts at the ticket desk, adjusting berets and counting her flock, while he is lugging cameras and large books, everything to complete and intensify the pupils' intellectual experience. But at the entrance, when the situation already seems perfectly clear, the malice of fate erupts: the thin, thuggish ticket collector runs at vulpine pace towards the male teacher. He stands across his path and asks in a placid tone, at the bottom of which promises of torment resound: 'Do you possess a photographic camera?'

'Yes, of course I do.'

'Aha. And have you read the sign beside the ticket desk?'

In his unfashionable trousers the teacher cringes, and the children nervously huddle in a flock: who knows what's going to leap out of the capital-city jungle next, what further injunction or lordly whim? The Varsovian eyes sparkle with spite, while the provincial eyes mist over with humiliation. The whole crowd heads off to look at the sign, while we go on to the elephants.

The Warsaw Zoological Garden occupies a large area. Why on earth must the two enormous elephants toddle about in a tiny little scrap of ground, bordered by spikes, wire-fenced and enclosed on all sides by rusted metal? In their baggy, penitential skins the elephants behave like saints amid the savage hoi polloi.

Not only do they not show anger towards their supervisors for this mortification, or towards the crowd for its exasperating gawking, or for its lack of faith in their great strength, but they even do their best to disarm the human beings with charm and docility. It's a wonder to gaze upon the gigantic bulk of their bodies, whose weight in itself is a murderous weapon, to see how meek they are, how they sway on their pillar-like legs with so much respect for the fragile barriers, for the trifling little spikes on the concrete wall above the ditch, for the very narrow moats, the tiny little arms and cowardly eyes. Why don't they use their jungle footsteps, swings and jumps to surpass man? Perhaps it's for exactly the same reason why saints don't use their divine strengths: they're waiting for the humans to let elephants be elephants and saints to be saints of their own accord, they're waiting for them to make way for superhuman matters and thus prove their humanity.

Unfortunately, they do not make way—on the contrary, they force the elephants into human habits, they offer them tiny apples and rolls on their tiny open palms. The elephants courteously deposit these dribs and drabs in the deep pit of their bellies, and one of them—more sanguine, more prone to despair, though no less patient than his companion—as a mark, perhaps, of self-irony, swallows each of these insubstantial gifts and then picks up a pile of rubbish with his trunk and scatters it on his head.

In the distance we can hear a roar, a single roar that intermittently changes into bleating. As if a bear and a ram were taking it in turns to roar. There's a throng in front of the cage, offering fruits and buns too, but here they're less of an affront to the potential scale of consumption. Sure enough, it's two bears. One of them is trotting the length of the front bars on down-at-heel paws, grabbing the food that's being thrown, while the other sits in the depths. It's this second one who is roaring, now fiercely, now like a ram—in the ultimate prostration. It's demanding treats with the wildest ursine greed and fears its larger cellmate with the most frantic, bestial terror. Now and then, while the big one is dawdling in the far corner, the small one furtively gallops to the bars, the humans get excited and shower it in a hail of apples, willing it to eat before the other one notices. Indeed, the poor wretch is trembling with eager desire, its eyes sink into its skull, it gathers speed—and suddenly sits back on its hind paws. No, it cannot overcome its fear. The pain of renunciation and its own disgrace tear at its throat: it groans and bleats like the devil. And no one knows who it is: is it a she-bear who's filled with sinister pleasure by this self-torment, this monstrous respect for the male primate? Or is it a weakling, a neurotic? Or simply an immature animal, doomed to the tyranny of a potentate? The humans are laughing, some are disconcerted, but no one is rebelling or shouting that this absurd constraint should immediately be withdrawn, and that the tragic conflict brought by cohabitation should be resolved at once.

One should really walk about the place, without scrutinizing the torments or the secrets of other creatures. Walking about the Warsaw zoo isn't very nice. One feels the same sort of anxiety as when wading around any nouveau-riche wilderness. Is there anyone in charge of the creative chaos? Will it all be shaped into harmony and order one day? Are they coping financially? Will they be able to catch up with the economic situation? Won't they lose the basic thread amid procrastination? The alleyways are scattered in cinder, the wide roads are disappearing in fine dust, there's grass overgrowing the paths and the lawns are shining with bald patches. Here and there the shapes of begonia beds choked with couch grass loom out. Spacious pits with taps and pipes set into the walls are dry, there are quagmires on the main roads, and all over the place there are hopeless, tacky temporary measures and abandoned works. A pool that's fit to perform its function is wire-fenced; a fine pavilion is boarded up; and right next to it some sheds are for the present too cramped, too stinky and too solid for short-term use.

The public at the Warsaw zoo looks impoverished and unimaginative. Few allow themselves to treat the animals, few are nicely dressed or have a carefree look on their faces. Dejected figures stop in front of the pens housing bizarre alien creatures, take a cursory glance into the depths of the cages, read the signs and walk away disappointed: is that all? A serval? An anteater? It has four legs, just like a dog or a pig. There's nothing in their eyes to suggest that a vision of the hot part of the world, a dream of another life, or the mystery of paradise has appeared to these visitors. The women usually voice their conjecture on whether or not the fur or skin they've just seen would make a lovely collar, and the men wonder how much food the foreign beast consumes per day, and how much it costs to keep. The Varsovians don't like to be surprised. If a person from the provinces or a child lets out a cry when faced by a fantastical creature, at once someone is sure to shoot it an angry look, hiss disdainfully or explain in a manner that doesn't allow for pipe dreams. Sometimes there's just a flash of resentment: a tail like that? A snout like that? Paws like nothing on earth? It's a disgrace to look at! And they walk on, scandalized.

Only the flamingos are apparently unable to offend anyone. It must be because these defenceless creatures flourish in a pink flock in the middle of an unfenced pond, because they're not very lively, far beyond the scale of animal life, they probably eat nothing, they're no use for anything and they don't exercise their wings to go anywhere. Various heavily built gentlemen who didn't twitch a muscle before the hyena's snout or before the beaks of the fabulous sapphire-blue parrots are alarmed here and say: 'What on earth are those things?! No, my God, what on earth are they?!'

Whereas no one's interested in the kangaroo. Neither what could be made out of it, nor how much it costs. It hops about its little meadow on its hind legs, not using its front paws at all, or lies in the grass like a badly folded object, a piece of junk of unknown use. A child asks: 'What's the meaning of this animal?' The mother replies: 'It's that it has to jump very far.' 'Then it can jump very far,' agrees the child and runs off to the monkeys. Clearly, too much specialization is off-putting.

The children and I go back to the serious animals, the beautiful, four-legged predators. They're divided according to species and according to age. The panthers are separate, so are the lions and tigers, and there's another cage with mixed youth: two lion cubs and two baby tigers. Emanating from all these iron bars is a sense of solemnity. The lives lived in there are no small matter and nothing in them comes from a fable by La Fontaine, as could be said of the bears or the elephants. The authors of fairy tales like to involve 'the king of the animals' in their educational plans, but the lion has no place in moral messages, not even when dressed in royal purple. I remember how I always bashfully overlooked any sort of allegory involving lions—they're too serious for insincerity. Children, who are themselves very serious, can sense this perfectly—and at once some proof appears. Here is a small boy of about five, playing with a baby lion. He's not playing flippantly, as one might play with a monkey, a dingo dog, a seal, a bear, or any wild but not serious animal. He's not throwing stones through the bars, he's not teasing it or making faces. There's no game-playing here. The boy and the lion looked at each other for the first time in their lives a minute ago. And they communicated. They certainly don't want to deceive, abuse, or annoy each other—they're not after entertainment; their aim is to confirm how much they concur and share the same feelings. When the boy hides around the corner of the adjoining building, the lion hides in a corner of the cage. Then the little boy runs out onto the path, his hair flying in the wind, he jumps up and down, runs as if set free from misfortune—and the lion races ahead too, as far as the space in its prison allows, and climbs onto its hind legs, leaping and prancing in elation. After that they run to and fro, steadily and soberly—this is solid field athletics training: the child goes up and down the path the length of the cage, the animal does the same inside it—they're in perfect step, persistently in rhythm. How similar they are—a fair, shaggy-maned, snub-nosed little boy with stern eyes and a very young animal, brotherly and bouncy!

The other lion cub doesn't join in with the fun: it has no partner, it hasn't found anyone among the humans to be its kindred spirit. It's sitting to one side, watching the other two's antics with a morose and knowing eye, without twitching a muscle. No, it's definitely not a desire for triumph or a need for thrills that's animating these two young creatures of different species—it's a lucky stroke of mutual understanding that's at work here. Above an unbounded ocean of differences, two hostile forces divided for centuries flow onto a wavelength of supreme harmony.

The baby tigers, however, have no concept of being adjuncts to a biological miracle: they'd like to grasp the meaning of their roommate's frolics, they've spotted that the boy is involved and that there's something curious and joyful going on. Childishly intrusive and foolish, they're scrambling near the inspired lion, getting in its way, nosing about, and doing the same as it is, like 'Father Virgil' in the children's song ('Hey there, children, hi de hi, hey there, do the same as I'). They're exercising their mental powers. But in vain! As it runs by, the lion cub strikes them with a paw and jumps over their backs, with its gaze fixed on those tiny green stars—the cat-like eyes of the gambolling little human.

Eventually the boy gets tired—he's fading. Whatever leonine quality he had in him, he has given back to the lion by now, and plainly the lion too has exhausted its human reserves. The child suddenly stops in mid-dance, and soon walks off at a different pace to the bench where his parents are sitting. And the lion lies down wearily too. A significant detail: neither of them turns their head to look back, there's no regret to be seen on either the lion's or the boy's face. Here is the advantage of children and animals over adults: friendship burns out entirely, without leaving any charred remains.

It's growing darker. The monkeys have settled on the highest ledge above their concrete-cased valley; they're throwing eggshells and peelings of some kind into the miserable stream at the bottom of it, they become pensive, make some faces, and finally, having forgotten the grand, cunning plan they started with, they jump down one at a time to fish out a half-eaten scrap. The sunset illuminates the monkeys' eyes as they crowd on the wall. How much more brightly the pupils of the Bandar-logs must have shone as they chattered on the roof of the temple! The Mazovian sun, incapable of striking a real spark out of subtropical creatures, is flowing all the more copiously over the peacocks' tails. The peacocks look happy with the climate. There's nothing in their bearing to imply the memory of a different motherland. Thanks to their excess of beauty and conceit that are alien in any conditions, they are not just foreign but literally unearthly, as if from another Earth, a richer and sillier planet.

Steering clear of their splendid tails, we head for the exit. The public is hurriedly floating away. Tired out, in a stained tunic, the 'lady animal doctor' is leaving the Tropical House in the company of an ugly, balding quadruped. The same people who reacted so insipidly to the extraordinary appearance of the anteater insistently block her way. 'What sort of an animal is that with you?' they ask time and again. 'It's a dog, it's a dog', she replies dryly.

Near the gate we stop again. How could one frigidly walk past what's going on at the top of the concrete cliff, in the vulture's nest? Above the heads of the passers-by, in the last rays of sunlight, shameless and sublime, the vultures are coupling. Hardly anyone stops; perhaps it doesn't occur to them that the painful screaming, those cruel blows, that lethal fracas between those large, tribal birds is love-making. The male vulture conquers the female and shakes his feathers. Immediately she gets up too, bleeding. They settle wing by wing, beaks turned towards the sun. At first they can't see anything, but soon their vulture gazes express astonishment…Astonishment combined with anger, filled with horror, so exalted that even in the human heart it stirs avian anxiety. What on earth is wrong? Why are the vultures so amazed? Maybe because the world hasn't changed…After such an onslaught, after such a cataclysm of love-making—the world hasn't changed!

We walk away. And like a lame, long-legged tramp, an eagle hobbles helplessly below the concrete cliff.

Past the gate we turn towards the Vistula, and soon we're on the large riverside common among some idly relaxing Varsovians. Among those who hadn't the desire, or hadn't the money, either for the zoo, or for the Kozłowski Brothers' private beach, or for 'a quick one', not even vinegar essence. Or else they didn't feel like it…Lying here are bachelors, young ladies, families and single mothers. There are children skipping around them as if among corpses. There's just as much litter here as in the monkeys' valley. And just as much fear, hatred and phoney humility as among the bears. Lots of redundant specialization. Some of their eyes are burning with a predator's solemnity…They're lying on the thin grass, without jackets, faces to the ground—rarely towards the sky, because the sky is boring and constantly asks questions. Here too love-making occurs. The couples sit hugging and looking woeful—afterwards they're amazed the world hasn't changed!

There's a soldier mooning about from one shakedown to the next. He's a watchman. With a rifle on his back he's guarding something—sweaty and morose, with his four-cornered cap pushed to the back of his head. So something has actually changed by the Vistula: formerly he'd have been a Russian soldier, but now he's Polish. A joyful change. After all, if one thinks about the friendship between the boy and the lion, or about the bloody encounter between the two enamoured vultures, it's hard to believe that a rifle, a uniform, or a national flag could denote one particular thing, could permanently delimit something or ward off anything definitive at all.

Icarus (1945)

Jarosław Iwaszkiewicz

There's a painting by Bruegel that bears the title 'Icarus'. If you look at this painting, you'll spot a peasant ploughing the land on a high seashore, a shepherd nonchalantly grazing his flock, a fisherman pulling his rods out of the sea, and a peaceful city in the distance. On the sea there's a ship in full sail, with some merchants discussing business on the deck. In short, we can see life with all its daily cares and the everyday strain of the usual human occupations and troubles. Where is Icarus? Where is the man who tried to fly to the sun? It's only when we examine the painting closely that in a corner of the sea we notice two legs sticking out of the water and some feathers floating in the air above it, yanked out of his cleverly constructed wings by the force of his dive. The fall of Icarus happened a moment ago. The daredevil who fitted himself with wings—according to the Greek legend—rose high, so high that he came near to the sun. The sun's rays melted the wax he had used to fix rows of feathers to his wings, and the young man fell. A tragedy occurred—here he is drowning, plunging into the sea, but the people in the picture haven't noticed. Neither the peasant ploughing the land, nor the merchant sailing into the distance, nor the shepherd staring into the sky—nobody saw the death of Icarus. Only the poet or the painter caught a glimpse of this death, and passed it on to posterity.

This painting always comes to my mind when I think about an experience I once had. It was June 1942 or 1943. A lovely summer's evening was settling on Warsaw, with radiant pink light casting decorative shadows on the ruined stone walls, as the forceful rush of people heading for home, hurrying to board the tram before the curfew, covered up the uniforms, already rare at this time of day, with a crowd of civilian clothing. If you were to look at the streets of Warsaw just then, full of life and beautiful in the June weather, for a while it might seem as if the city were free of its invader. For a while...

I was standing on the corner of Trębacka Street and Krakowskie Przedmieście, at the tram stop. Sonorously ringing their bells, the trams were lining up their big red hulks one behind the other the length of Krakowskie Przedmieście. Droves of people were packing themselves into them, thronging on the steps, standing on the buffers and hanging in clusters from the back and sides. Now and then a red 'zero' flashed by, reserved for Germans only, and thus almost empty. I was having to wait a rather long time for a tramcar that could be boarded easily. And as soon as one finally came along, I didn't feel like getting into it; all of a sudden I developed a taste for the crowd surrounding me, only paying the most casual heed to my existence. In front of me, high on his pedestal stood the national bard, Adam Mickiewicz; around the monument modest flowers were blooming, fragrant in spite of all, cars were grating their way around the corner before the Carmelite church, boys were selling newspapers with loud shouts, pedlars with cigarettes and biscuits were teeming outside a glistening shop, shutters were noisily being closed and bars drawn across store windows and doors; in a small garden, its benches filled to the very last space by old and young, sparrows were twittering, equally densely settled on some spindly little trees—all this was slowly sinking into the blue murk of a summer's evening. At that very moment I could hear the beating heart of Warsaw, and I found myself lingering among the people, just to spend a little longer in their company, and in company with them to savour this urban summer's evening.

At some point I noticed a youth who, coming from the direction of Bednarska Street, rather rashly stepped out from behind the red hull of a tram that was already moving; as he stood on a small traffic island with his face to the roadway and his back to the traffic, his eyes remained glued to the book with which he had emerged from the fading twilight. He was fifteen, at most sixteen years old. As he read, from time to time he shook his flaxen mane to brush aside the hair that kept falling on his brow. With one book protruding from his side pocket, and another held before his eyes, he was evidently incapable of tearing his gaze from it. He must have only just obtained it from a friend, or at a clandestine library, and without waiting to get home, was eager to acquaint himself with its contents there and then, in the street. I was sorry I didn't know what sort of a book it was—from a distance it looked like a textbook, but perhaps no textbook could arouse such interest in a young person. Maybe it was poetry? Maybe a book on economics? I don't know.

For a while he continued to stand on the island, engrossed in reading. He took no notice of the jostling, of the crowd pushing on board the tramcars. A few red streaks went past behind him, but still he kept his eyes glued firmly to the book. And still with that book under his nose—whether tired of the jostling and shouting around him, or suddenly subconsciously aware of the need to hurry home—I saw him step off the island into the roadway, straight under an approaching car.

The rasp of slammed-on brakes rang out and the screech of tyres on asphalt; to avoid running the boy down, the car had veered aside abruptly and come to a sudden halt right on the corner of Trębacka Street. To my horror I noticed that it was a Gestapo van. The youth with the book tried to go past it, but just at that moment the doors at the back of the van opened and two individuals in helmets with death's head insignia jumped out into the road. They landed right beside the boy. One of them screamed in a hoarse voice, as the other made a circular hand motion, sneeringly inviting him inside.

To this day I can still see the youth standing by the van door, disconcerted, quite simply abashed...shying away with a negative, naïve shake of the head, like a child promising never to do it again... 'I've done nothing,' he seemed to be saying, 'I was just...' He was pointing at the book, as the reason for his lack of attention. As if in this situation something could be explained. With the final impulse of his ruined life he was refusing to get into the van.

The gendarme demanded to see the boy's papers, seized the Kennkarte he proffered and violently pushed him inside. The other one helped him, the boy sat down, the Gestapo men followed, the doors crashed shut and the van took off at speed, heading rapidly towards their headquarters on Szuch Avenue.

It disappeared from sight. I looked around me, in search of common understanding, some fellow feeling for what had just happened here. After all, the youth with the book was done for. To my utter amazement I realized that nobody else had noticed the incident. Everything I have described occurred so quickly, at such lightning speed, and everyone in the crowded street was so involved in his own haste that the youth's abduction had gone unnoticed. The ladies standing right beside me were arguing over which tram would be more convenient for their journey, two gentlemen behind the tram stop were lighting cigarettes, a granny beside a basket set against the wall kept repeating over and over: 'Lemons, lemons, lovely lemons', like a Buddhist mantra, while some other young men ran across the street after departing tramcars, risking being hit by other vehicles... As Mickiewicz went on standing there quietly, the flowers continued to give off their scent, and the small birches and rowan trees beside the monument rustled in the gentle breeze, that fellow's disappearance meant nothing to anyone. I alone had noticed that Icarus had drowned.

I went on standing there for a long time, waiting for the crowd to grow thinner. It occurred to me that perhaps 'Michaś'—as I called him in my mind—would come back.

I imagined his home, his parents expecting his return, his mother getting the supper ready, and I refused to admit the thought that they'd never find out how their son had perished. Knowing the habits of our invaders, I didn't believe he could get out of their grip. And he had fallen into it in such a stupid way! The mindless cruelty of that abduction moved me to the quick, and still does to this day.

Those who were killed in battle, those who knew what they were dying for, may have found consolation in the fact that their death had some meaning. But how many there were like my Icarus, who drowned in the sea of oblivion for a cruelly mindless reason.

Evening came, and the city began to sink into a feverish, sickly sleep...Finally I moved away from my tram stop, passed the Mickiewicz monument, and went home on foot. But in my mind I was still pursued by the image of Michaś shaking his head, as if to say: 'No, no, it's just this book that's to blame...I'll be careful from now on...'

Traces (1946)

Ludwik Hering

They come out at night, taking advantage of the darkness and of smuggling opportunities close to the wall. They slip through holes and gaps in the gutters you'd think too narrow for a cat to pass through. If the adults give them a leg up to get on top of the wall, they land on this side like cats.

That's what people call after them in the city: 'A cat! A cat!', and it has come to mean the same as the word '*Jude*'. A patchwork of mud and fear. Concealed in the gloom, the sense of the approaching day: hounded beggar children.

Lurking until dawn on the street mortified by the ghetto and cemetery wall, they take advantage of the first early-morning traffic to weave in among the labourers and flit off to districts further away from the ghetto.

They want to get as far as possible from the wall—not even a zealous policeman will turn them back from there. Why would he bother to make the long journey to Gęsia Street for nothing and waste precious time that's rich in more profitable opportunities—such as an adult Jew, for instance?

All of the least fallible canine psychology encapsulated in the eyes of a defenceless child: dodge, stop, flee.

Those eyes in the haggard little faces—alert, wary, vigilant—those eyes protect but often betray them.

A child cowering against a wall, cornered by his Aryan peers, doesn't defend himself, he doesn't bite or kick. He keeps quiet amid a chorus of insults, trying to cast his gaze over the heads of his assailants, watching out for another danger: a uniform.

He waits, until bored by his passivity they slacken the ring. On he goes, dragging his feet behind him in disintegrating bast shoes and rags—the very thin shinbones thickened by the knots of his buckling knees.

They cover a hundred streets, a hundred floors. They knock at door after door. Or else, out of strength, half asleep, resigned, entirely heedless, they sit in the alcoves of gateways and shops.

They come back in the evening, groaning with exhaustion. They rattle their tins and hold up their coat tails with care, the linings artfully filled with begged food.

Even the children who have no one left to return to go back behind the wall. In summer, when it's warm, some of them spend the night in sheds by the clay ponds, in ruined houses or under the open sky in suburban fields.

Maybe the fact that they keep returning gives them relative impunity.

In winter they come back for the warmth. Within the ghetto, the floorboards were torn out of the corridors long ago, as were the window frames on the staircases, the balustrades, stair rails, and often the stairs themselves for firewood. But within the ghetto every cranny of every hallway and cellar is packed with people. Crowded in the corners, they keep each other warm with their own body heat. In the morning the stronger ones scramble out from under the semi-corpses and corpses to survive one more day beyond the wall. Most of them are the only providers for their family.

Towards evening they come trailing along the streets from various parts of the city—limping, ungainly, like injured birds returning to their nests.

They gather in large swarms by the gateways leading beyond the wall. They stand for hours in the freezing cold, scorching heat or rain, waiting for a capricious nod from the guards, as indifferent as stone idols.

Sometimes, tired of waiting, they organize a group offensive, advancing in a swarm and breaking through a convoy.

They push 'persistently', 'insolently' and 'impudently'.

They jump up and jump away—hoarse and weary. Avoiding spiteful little urchins, they carefully hold up the tails of their coats, like heavy clumps of the promised land, stuffed with the bread and potatoes they've begged.

Quite often, on the orders of a gendarme they're forced to throw these fruits of their all-day labour onto a heap, into the mud by the wall, and then go inside with nothing under a hail of truncheon and rifle-butt blows.

* * *

He's about six years old. He's sitting on a stool, his little blue hands embracing a steaming mug. He's wrapped like a mummy in a worn-out scarf that's tied on his back in a careful knot. He's reclining his head of a very young pharaoh, too heavy for his slender neck, with large, protruding ears. His long, bulging eyelids readily droop on eyes that are now off duty. Two subtle lines the length of the nose to the mouth add definition to the translucent little face with the proud expression of someone initiated into adult suffering.

He explains firmly: 'I refuse to lie. I'm already eight years old.

'Before the war a child was born to us. Daddy was a barber—and as you do at work, some days he'd eat this, some days that, not always kosher. And our child died.

'Why should I say I'm six when I'm eight? For the Lord God to take revenge on me?'

He talks in a feeble, singsong voice, drawing out his final words. There's no doubt in anything he says. There may be things he can't accept, but there's nothing that surprises him.

In a matter-of-fact tone he says: 'The main thing is not to swell up, because that's the end. And to avoid swelling up you have to eat at least once a day. But what can we use to buy food now, when everything we had has been sold?

'When nothing was left but the bed and the quilt, Mummy just cried and cried, and she kept uncovering my legs to see if they were starting to swell.

'What's the use of crying?

'And over there no one will give us anything. Here, on this side, people are less stingy than in there. There each person thinks only of himself—even within the family. My father's sister and her children live with us. It's all right for them! There's a boy of sixteen already, and he trades. But they argue too, because he cheats her. Once I saw him at a shop, eating two Graham bread rolls and thirty grams of dripping. Maybe fifty.

'There's such a crush in that shop each morning! The smugglers come there to eat and drink tea. They drink vodka too. I used to go there to gather crumbs from the table, but you can't gather many crumbs, can you? And stronger boys come along and push you away. There's so much bread there! *Beutelbrot* and sifted rye and rolls, even *leykukh*: large yellow slabs of it, and you get two in a stack, like bricks, so they're all but sagging.

'One time I just stood and sniffed, I went on sniffing until I fell asleep. When I woke up I was lying there, in the mud. And then I washed and washed...so Mummy wouldn't know. She's always doing the laundry, though only in water. She's always afraid about getting lice and about swelling up.

'So I've started going outside the wall, like the other kids. What scares me the most is the urchins. But now I'm wise: I keep a few groszy in my pocket, and I hide the rest well. If they attack me, they'll only take a small sum. Anyway, it's quite hard to recognize me, 'cos I'm not as dirty as the other kids, Mummy sees to that. For a time they did recognize me because I had the "wrong" hat. What I'm the most afraid of when it's dark in the ghetto is treading on a corpse. When it's covered with paper you can see it from a distance, but not otherwise.

'I go out through a hole under the wall, but not on the way back, because lots of policemen hang around there, and I have to go to the guard post on Gęsia Street. Sometimes I come back earlier, when there aren't any other kids yet, and look to see if there's a decent German.

'How can you tell? What do you mean? By the eyes! But it's hard to get it right, and I make mistakes too: I go up, and what a kick he gives me!'

A tabby kitten has been stalking under the stove for some time, and suddenly pounces on the child's trailing shoe lace. The little boy smiles—he puts down the pot, slowly bends over, sighing with the effort, picks up the kitten and settles it on his lap.

'We had a cat too. We had everything—even an electric teaspoon.

'If Daddy were alive things'd be different now—but how can Mummy cope on her own?

'Last night it was windy—Mummy couldn't sleep and she heard the attic window flapping. She quickly got up to go and take the food pushed through it, but at once other people flocked in—they shoved her aside and someone else took it. She screamed that it wasn't fair because she'd heard it first, but what's the use? You need a strong person in there.

'My daddy was tough. He used to whirl me round outside the shop: I'd hold onto a stick, Daddy would spin it in a circle and I'd fly in the air. But one time I let go, I fell down and didn't know what was happening. When I woke up there was such a loud scream! and I had to reassure them there was nothing wrong with me.

'Whenever I walk past the spot, I can hardly believe all that really happened. Sometimes I'm so tired, so tired, and

I think how good life was that time when I fell and couldn't feel a thing.

'Once I met a man on Grójecka Street. He was standing on his own at a stop, and the street was still entirely empty. The way he looked at me, I was scared to walk past. He must be a bad man, I thought to myself. I was afraid to turn and run away, so I went up to him and didn't beg, I just asked politely what time it was. And then very, very slowly, slowly walked away. But I could hear him running after me—and I felt even more afraid. But for no reason. He came up, took hold of me (he really did grab hold of me!) and carried me off to his house. He gave me breakfast, a bath, and put me to bed (he really did put me to bed!), and I fell asleep. When I woke up, it was late—I couldn't go home any more so I had to stay the night.

'I told him I'd thought he must be bad. He was so surprised he went red. "Did you really think that? Really?", he said, and then "Maybe that's right." But it wasn't—he was definitely a good man.'

The child's smile fades very slowly, splayed out on wrinkles of suffering.

'But that night I was so frightened by being away from home that I couldn't sleep at all. I'll never spend the night on the outside again. I'm afraid of something serious happening at home when I'm not there.'

Now he's gone back at the right time.

* * *

One night no children came out from behind the wall. In June 1942 the Grossaktion to deport everyone from the ghetto had started.

The guard posts along the wall were reinforced. Hirelings in uniform, black with web belts, were densely deployed, Latvians apparently. Behind the wall the Aktion continued. Shots were fired into the air, summoning people to come out of their houses. Screaming and crying were audible, and the din of the seething crowd gathered for 'selection'. And the dry crack of isolated shots to liquidate those lying on the ground. Straight into the cobblestones. The rattle of machine guns never fell silent.

At the head of Stawki Street, all day long in scorching heat, a teeming lava of half-alive people flowed in the direction of the railway sidings, where the goods trains were waiting in strings.

In a chorus of groaning multiplied by the terror in thousands of eyes, they were shut with a clang into railcars stinking of chlorine.

Time after time, the cemetery gate and the guard-post gate opposite flung their wings open and brought them together again. Groups of horror-stricken people were being herded behind their see-through steel barriers to be executed.

At night, the rattle audible from there never ceased for an instant—in the morning the Jewish policemen used watering cans to rinse off the driveway, awash with blood that had leaked from the carts, and then scattered a thick layer of sand on the cobbles to soak up the red liquid.

And sometimes smaller units earmarked for a transport were let out through there.

Once, as one of these clusters of women was being swiftly herded along, a German from the guard post separated a toddler from its mother. The mother was yanked into a group being chivvied down Okopowa Street.

From the ghetto gates, the wall continues in a straight line for about a hundred paces, then it turns a slight curve and blocks the view.

This woman was walking backwards, looking at the child. She tripped and fell. Kicked by a German, she picked herself up and walked on, still backwards, keeping pace with the unit as it was herded along, but without tearing her eyes from the gate. A hundred paces—then the wall turns.

* * *

It's snowing. The flat, white landscape of the ghetto is rippled by lumpy pink heaps of crushed rubble. Here and there the broken shinbones of rails and iron structures protrude. At Stawki Street a rusty cornfield of beds dragged out of non-existent houses is turning red, with a cap of snow on top. Lower down, patches of earth full of pots and bowls under a slippery load of falling snow take on colour. In the silence, garish enamel makes a ticking noise as it crackles in the frost. There's a sound of metal rims scraping together: it's a man wrenching a baby pram free of a tangle of dried stalks.

The wall and gate opposite the cemetery lie collapsed under the snow. Through a large hole into a playing field next to the cemetery children can be seen sledging down mounds of earth that didn't fit in the filled-up ditches.

Words and laughter bounce like balls off walls mutilated by firing squads.

The graves are silent after rippling for three days, shouting for three days, before they came to a stop.

The space—wounded by the gaze of the mother torn from her child—is not bleeding.

Fine, heavy snow is falling. The sky, the earth and the flattened ghetto are quivering like the print on a disintegrating page.

The Funeral
(1947)

Zofia Petersowa

The slight, modest figure known as nothing more personal than Adamowa—'the wife of Adam'—was of so little concern to the residents of the apartment house that they simply nodded when they heard the news of her death.

'Oh dear, so the old girl has died. The doctor's wife gave her a pretty good life, she's a human being, she had respect for the old servant.'

Mrs Oseniowa, as the doctor's wife was called, lived on the second floor, where she had rented out three of her rooms, while accommodating herself quite comfortably in the remaining two. In the past, when her husband was still alive, she had lived in considerable luxury, but now the war was gradually taking away her valuable furniture, the paintings gone dark with a patina of time, the heavy family silver, the Slutsk sashes, once resplendent with brightly coloured silks, the real Persian rugs, the rare porcelain, bronzes, tapestries and costly trinkets. Nonetheless, those two rooms were still crammed with impressive pieces of old mahogany and ash-wood furniture, while Meissen and Sèvres groups danced flirtatiously in the glass-fronted cabinets and on the shelves, cut glass glittered like a rainbow in the sun, and ladies in hundred-year-old hair styles and gentlemen in stock ties smiled out of the miniatures.

Mrs Oseniowa did not maintain a wide range of contacts. A few close female friends from long ago and a couple of grey-haired gentlemen called on her from time to time. Otherwise, she and Adamowa lived quietly among the valuable mementoes and knick-knacks.

It was Adamowa who polished and dusted them. She had worked for the doctor's wife for twenty years, helping to raise both her sons, and she was regarded as a member of the family. Mrs Oseniowa could probably have eaten a little better, or occasionally spent money on a new dress, because her pre-war ones were falling apart by now, but Adamowa would not let her waste a penny.

'Why do we need that? Can't we eat like others? We'll lose a bit of weight, but there'll be more things left for the boys. You're not thinking of them at all! You just want to spend money! It's healthier for us to go without meat anyway, and we've had plenty of fat all our lives, so a Lenten diet won't hurt us. You should get rid of some of the junk. Any of the commission stores would take our things.'

And the doctor's wife yielded. In the hands of the old servant money stretched like rubber, and although the soups she made were thin and monotonous, they rarely had to sell anything.

'Zbyszek is so fond of this dinner service!' the old woman would go on as she dusted in the glass-fronted cabinet. 'And Ksawery was always playing with this knife when he was little,' she said, picking up a dagger with a hilt set with gemstones.

Mrs Oseniowa sighed heavily. Adamowa's words gave her courage and the hope that her sons would come home. Both were in a concentration camp. Now and then a laconic card in German came from one of them, and then the women made up a parcel and sent it to the camp. So far, both were alive, but throughout the city the mothers were going about in tears, the wives were being notified that their husbands were dead, the fiancées, sisters, and all the other women were in great uncertainty about their loved ones' future. And so very many of them had stopped writing to their families.

'It's all right. They're holding out!' Adamowa comforted her as they sat darning and patching by the harsh, narrow glow of the carbide lamp. 'But I've heard the Krauts are after medical equipment now. They have lists of doctors so they're swiping their instruments. But don't they have enough of it at the front? We should keep ours for Zbyszek. Ksawery's compasses are another desirable item. Those devils can take the lot and the children will lose it all.'

'What if we hide it in the cellar?'

'Hm, it's damp down there. Anyway, aren't they sure to search under the coal?'

The old dear spent so much time worrying about those things for the boys she had raised that it must have been the worrying that caused her death; she hadn't been ill at all. It happened at some point in late July, 1944.

The weather was extremely hot. For several weeks they were left alone in the flat, because the tenants had gone on holiday. The women rarely went out, and in any case the city was not a safe place to be. There was something ominous in the air. From the Praga direction an unbroken string of troops was heading west into the centre; all the bridges and streets were jammed with trains, cars, horses, tanks, Red Cross vans, cannons, carts and lorries. The rumour was that the Germans were retreating along the entire front line, but despite caution on the part of the authorities, news was trickling through to the population, finding confirmation in the troop movement.

Everyone in the house went to see the march-past. Some bought rugs, revolvers, or even horses and carts from the stragglers. The Hungarians in particular were selling everything they had. News of the bargains on offer ran through the city, prompting many people to hurry along to get something from the soldiers. So no one was especially interested in the fact that old Adamowa had died, or maybe they simply didn't hear about it.

One evening a coffin was delivered. Mrs Oseniowa went down to see the concierge and asked to be issued with a document confirming that Adamowa had lived in this house.

'My brother-in-law has already called by to issue the death certificate,' she said, 'but at the cemetery they're asking for confirmation of her address too.'

'I'll bring it up to you right away,' said the concierge. 'And I'll take a look at the deceased.'

'Oh, my dear Mrs Kowalska, we've already had to close the coffin. The smell was so bad it was getting hard to bear.'

'Well, it's awful hot; bodies have a way of decomposing, as we know,' the concierge lectured her. 'But at least we must say our prayers.'

She came up, had a look at the coffin, crossed herself and was gone. Well? Adamowa was old, and so she died. No wonder. There wasn't time to go to the funeral, because it was a Saturday, there were the steps to be washed, the cleaning to be done, and then she had to fly off and watch the Germans running away. In any case, the doctor's wife did not need anybody else. Her husband's brother, also a doctor, and her sister-in-law helped her with it all; various documents were obtained, permissions and stamps, Mrs Oseniowa went to Powązki Cemetery and bought a grave, the hearse arrived, the coffin was put inside it and the family took the deceased to the cemetery.

But she clearly felt sad in the empty flat, because a week later she went away to her in-laws in Radom, and only the lodgers were left in the flat. She undoubtedly won out by doing so, because she spent the entire Uprising outside Warsaw.

She returned home in April of the next year. Warsaw was still piled with heaps of rubble. It was black with charred ruins and red with bricks ripped from the insides of houses. Like bones protruding from their torsos, girders, singed planks and metal bars blocked every passage, creating a tangle of wires, toppled lamp posts, shattered paving stones, roofs and trusses, pieces of internal walls, marble and stucco, broken doors and windows, the remains of bath tubs and smashed-up stoves. The streets were like fantastical fallow ground where in between the borders of the empty blackened skeletons that had once been houses, winding paths climbed and writhed, either to the height of each storey or through bomb holes. The sky showed straight through the collapsed interiors of the apartment houses, and only here and there was an abandoned stove still standing, attached to a piece of brick wall. Dust filled one's eyes and forced its way into one's throat and lungs, one's feet had difficulty finding a flat surface and twisted on the rubble. From every direction came citizens returning to their unfortunate capital. Some had bundles, but most were empty-handed, ragged, dirty, exhausted, weeping or silent, walled in by pain. On squares large and small, on every flat surface, in courtyards and on the high edges of monstrous bomb craters small burial mounds protruded, unmarked or supplied with provisional crosses, telling the tale of the city's historic tragedy. The odour of putrefaction, of soot, burned paper and timber hung motionless in the air. Not even the wind could drive it away; it was coming from the houses, from the stone walls, from caved-in cellars full of corpses, from the melting remains of mud and snow, from rotting, blood-soaked rags and from the carcasses of dogs and horses.

People were saying that on one or another street the entrance to a house had been dug out, and its annex was still standing; they were telling stories of charred corpses in gateways and courtyards, of whole floors that had survived with no staircase, or of strange twists of fate that had kept someone's flat intact, though wrecked and destroyed inside. Besides the thousands of citizens returning, the most noticeable sight was the horde of people in navy-blue or blue striped gowns, heavily patched or plain ragged; they were dirty, louse-infested, so thin and with such sallow complexions that it was as if the corpses had emerged from under the collapsed buildings and were trailing through their home city like ghosts: these were the prisoners whom the march of victorious troops had freed from the concentration camps. They had walked for days and nights, stealing or begging, in the hope of finding their loved ones among the ruins of Warsaw. As they searched the rubble, the wind yanked at their wretched, skinny figures, as if trying to carry them away.

Mrs Oseniowa entered the city with a small group from the Bielany district in the north, and headed for home. She wept as she looked at the dreadful destruction, sank into holes and heaps of rubble, picked her way out of dug-up ditches, disentangled herself from barbed wire, fell over, stood up and trudged onwards. Just one more turn—she barely recognized which street was which—just a bit further. Yes, wasn't the pharmacy here? An oak tree lay shattered before her, and there were no houses at all, as if nothing had ever been here but heaps of bricks. She was afraid to turn the corner of a nearby building that stood black with soot, majestic in its destruction: behind it was the apartment house in which she lived. Or rather it had been there. But was it still there?

From behind the black, burned-out hull of the five-storey building she peeped into the cross street, and a surge of joy filled her face with a blush: the apartment house was standing. Not only was it standing, but there were people bustling around it, lifting charred floorboards, carrying bricks onto piles and removing rubble.

Everyone helped each other. Water was fetched from the Vistula in dented buckets or in surviving pots and pans; thanks to their joint efforts a fire was kept going in the courtyard, where together they cooked food, as they carried on tidying. After two nights spent sleeping on the rubble with nothing but a threadbare overcoat to cover her, the doctor's wife was in the same condition as all the other citizens, but she went on working zealously. No one could have imagined that this sixty-year-old woman could muster so much resilience, have so much strength and be quite so provident.

A few days later she had reached the point where she had a straw mattress in the sitting room, then she fetched a stool from the cellar, a chipped bowl, a pot and a chest, which she made into a table. She had a little money, so she bought some food from the local market traders and waited. She was waiting for her sons.

Her brother-in-law and his wife appeared. They tried to persuade the stubborn creature to go back to Radom with them, but all their arguments came to nothing.

'How will they know where their mother has gone?'

'You must give the neighbours our address. Or you could write it on the walls. The boys'll come home, read the message and come to Radom.'

'But what for? Will they have the strength to do that? No, let them find me here,' she insisted.

And she stuck to her guns. One day, both her sons came back, darkened by poverty and starving like the rest, but alive and whole.

Mrs Oseniowa thought that was right and proper. She bustled about briskly, laundering the boys' rags, patching them as best she could, and feeding her sons whatever she could get from the tradeswomen who crowded the edges of the streets and the stalls on the cleared squares.

'Once you've had a good rest we'll go to Radom.'

'What's going to happen now?' wondered Zbyszek. 'Where can we go for aid? You don't have that much money, Mama. Who can give us some clothes? Where should we start?'

'Don't worry about it. You'll just have to stick it out a little longer. Everything's going to be fine. The government has already moved from Lublin to Warsaw. You must both enrol for the university, because you have to finish your degrees.'

They looked at their mother in surprise and exchanged knowing winks. Poor old thing: all this misfortune is making her spout nonsense. University? In these ruins? In

Kraków, perhaps? But how would they get there? And where would they get the money for their studies?

One day Mrs Oseniowa went out, while the two boys, still feeling weak, stayed at home. Zbyszek was making soup, and Ksawery was dozing on the straw mattress when a militiaman entered the room.

'Citizens, please come with me.'

They stared at him in amazement, unable to understand what this was about, because he did not seem very official. He sat down on the stool and started scratching his head under his cap.

'Where do you want us to go?'

'It's a nasty business, citizens. It's about Mother.'

'Mother? Our mother?'

'So it seems. Here it clearly says "Mrs Oseniowa, widow of Dr Henryk Oseń". And the address is in order.'

Zbyszek read the card; yes, it was about their mother.

'But what's happened? Where's our mother?' they asked, pulling on their clothes.

'Well... she's at the cemetery.'

'Whaaat?' Zbyszek froze with his jacket halfway over his head, and Ksawery sat up on the straw mattress and let his jaw drop, forgetting the boot he was lacing.

'It's because Mrs Oseniowa is, er... a little, as it were... Well, she's gone mad or something!' blurted the militiaman.

'Oh my God!'

Moments later they were outside. The boys took off at such speed that the militiaman could hardly keep up with them.

'The police station was informed that a woman—no one knew her name—was digging up a grave at the cemetery. The chief sent two of us to investigate. We arrived, and found it was true! There was a crowd of people trying to explain to her that it's not allowed, but she kept insisting there was no corpse buried there, and she had to dig up the coffin. She didn't look like a madwoman, so we checked her identity, but she kept repeating that there was no deceased in the grave, that she was fit and well, that she wouldn't leave the grave, and she asked for her sons to come. So we conferred, went back to the police station, sent for the prosecutor, and now I've come to fetch you.'

They dashed through the Powązki Cemetery gate and turned down a side path. From a distance, between the tombstones they could see a crowd of people standing around one of the graves.

Mrs Oseniowa was hot and bothered, and the prosecutor was sitting facing her on a roadside pillar, asking her questions, to which she was replying in a controlled but exasperated tone. Two militiamen were holding back the small crowd that was pushing forwards in curiosity.

'Mama, what's happened?'

'Ah, here you are at last! Please tell them I'm in my right mind. I must dig up this grave, I must, for your sakes. There's no dead body in here.'

'Would you gentlemen please give me your personal details? Is this your mother?'

'Absolutely!' said Zbyszek, putting his arm around her. 'What's going on here?'

The prosecutor looked at their gaunt young faces, which were the picture of astonishment. The boys were in concentration-camp striped uniforms and their heads were shaved.

'Mr Prosecutor,' said Ksawery at last, 'our mother's as fit as a fiddle. If she's got it into her head to dig up a grave, she must know what she's doing. But I don't understand... What's in there, Mama, if as you say Adamowa isn't buried here?'

Mrs Oseniowa waved her hands indignantly.

'I can't tell you right now because there are too many people here. Mr Prosecutor, please allow me to go on digging. But only when all these onlookers have gone!'

The prosecutor's young, cheerful face expressed interest.

'All right, then. Would the Citizen Militiamen please remove the crowd? Yes... back off, please, and some more... Please be on your way. You're not at the theatre!

We'll wait a while,' he said, addressing the silent, confused boys, 'but I warn you that if your mother is found to be misleading the authorities, she'll face serious consequences. However, if it turns out events have caused her to need medical treatment, you gentlemen will have to take care of her.'

'Mr Prosecutor,' shouted Mrs Oseniowa, spreading her arms, 'you'll soon see for yourself!'

Meanwhile, the militiamen and the cemetery caretakers had dispersed the curious crowd.

'Please dig up the grave,' said the prosecutor, walking up to it.

The spades bit into the mound. Two more shovels were fetched, and both boys started to help. Heaps of fresh earth rose higher and higher on either side as the diggers plunged deeper and deeper into the pit. Up flew the earth, falling in brown cascades and the polished surfaces of the spades flashed, until finally the coffin lid thudded beneath the workers' feet. Some webbing straps were fetched.

'Lower, lower!'

'Put them under the corners! Deeper...'

The diggers threw the ends of the straps out of the pit, scrambled up and took hold of them on either side of the grave.

'All together! Steady does it! Again...and again...'

Up came the coffin, until finally its black, earth-strewn lid appeared. The reverse order of events had the surprising effect of bringing back remote sorrows. A shudder of horror and of tense anticipation ran through the company. Now the coffin was beside the grave, and the straps supporting it were dropped.

'It's soldered shut, Mr Prosecutor. We've nothing to open it with,' reported the militiaman.

'I've got some tools here! They might do the job,' said Mrs Oseniowa, fetching a large suitcase from behind the neighbouring tomb. Beside some sacks and cords, a hatchet, several chisels and some hammers appeared. 'At the very worst we'll have to carve a hole in the lid.'

'No, the lid must remain intact,' replied the prosecutor, shifting his gaze from the coffin to the grey-haired, preoccupied woman. He was plainly doubtful but also curious.

'It'll be done in a jiffy!' declared one of the workmen, as they hit the side of the coffin with the hammers. As the chisels rasped away, pieces of wood snapped. 'It's wooden, Mr Prosecutor, only the edge is metal. It's gone completely soft already and it's giving way easily. Just the top and bottom to go and we'll be there.'

'All together now! All together! Up, up! That's it!'

They gathered closely around the coffin as the lid slowly went up. First it rose by a hand's width, then higher and higher, until finally it was lying on the heap of earth. The contents of the coffin were covered by a black cloth, tightly tucked in at the edges. The militiaman leaned forwards, took hold of it with both hands and tugged.

Indescribable amazement shone from their faces: under the material lay a fur coat.

'What's this?!' said the prosecutor, frowning and rubbing his eyes. 'What does it mean?'

'I told you there wasn't a corpse in here,' replied Mrs Oseniowa triumphantly, and kneeled beside the coffin. She picked up the fur coat and reached inside. 'Here you are,' she said, extracting a saffian leather case, 'this is my silver. And here,' she said, handing Ksawery a small box, 'are your compasses. I saved your father's surgical instruments from the Germans for you too, Zbyszek,' she added, overturning and searching among the various tightly packed objects.

The gilded frame of a painting flashed, the brocade of an old tablecloth shone, the inlay on an elaborate casket sparkled.

'As God is my witness,' one of the militiamen couldn't help saying, 'I doubt anything like this has ever happened before!'

'But where's Adamowa?' spluttered Zbyszek in amazement.

'Adamowa? She's in Radom!' said his mother, turning to face him. 'She packed it all herself with her own hands before she left.'

Silence fell.

The prosecutor merely shook his head.

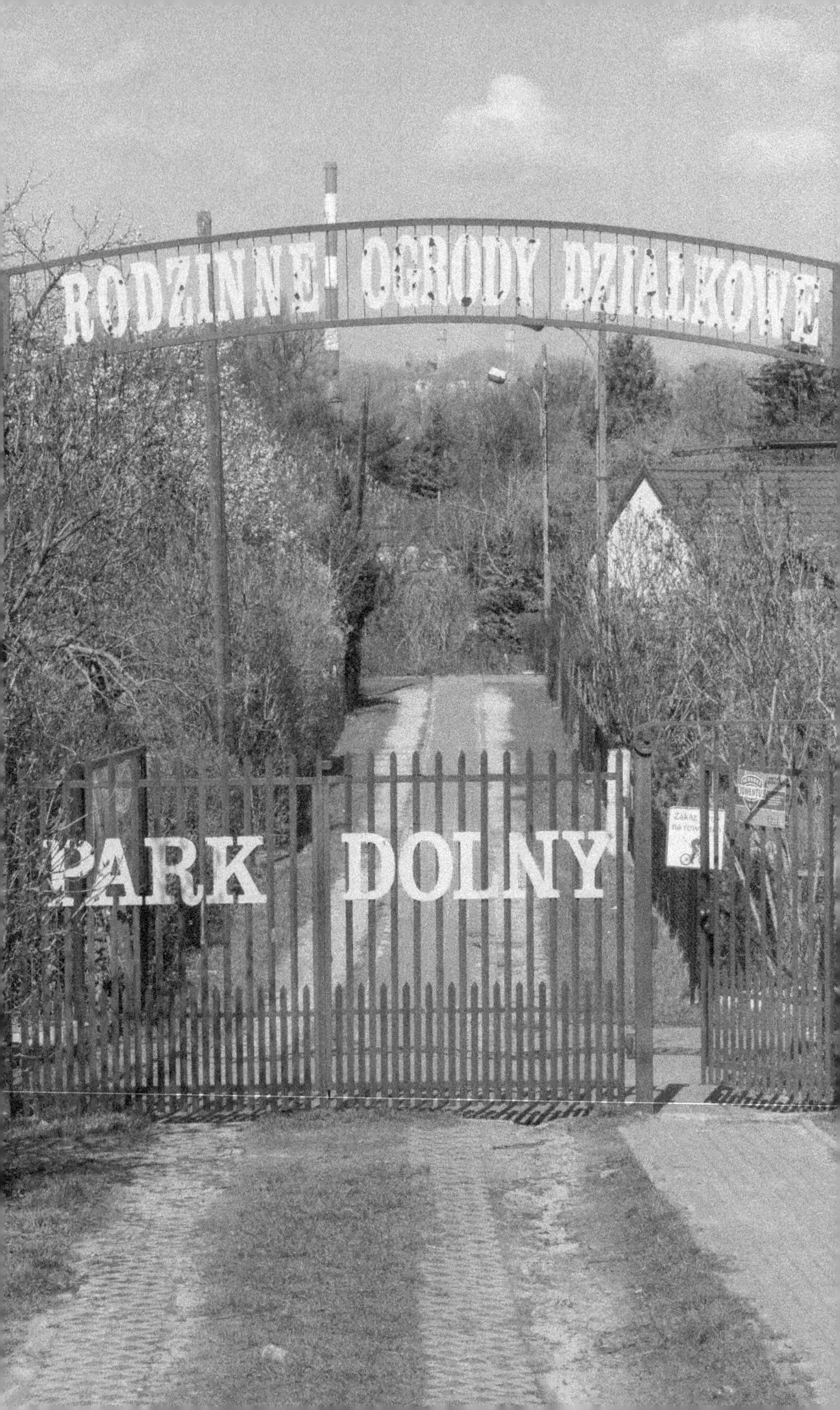
RODZINNE OGRODY DZIAŁKOWE
PARK DOLNY

First Step in the Clouds (1956)

Marek Hłasko

On Saturdays the city centre looks much the same as on any other day of the week. Except there are more drunks; in the pubs and bars, on the buses and in gateways—simply everywhere there's a smell of half-digested alcohol in the air. On Saturdays the city loses its hard-worker's face—on Saturdays it has the ugly mug of a drunk. Meanwhile on Saturdays there are none of those people in the city centre who like to watch life go by: they stand around in gateways, trail about the streets or sit on park benches for hours on end, merely to be able to recall in twenty years' time that on such and such a day they saw a more or less unusual incident. Just like the messengers who were still going about in their red hats during the occupation, just like the dealers in dry sand, or the buskers singing in a tipsy tenor—in the city centre the objective observers of life have died out now.

Observers of this kind can only be encountered in the suburbs. Life in the suburbs is and always has been more compact; in the suburbs, every Saturday when the weather is fine people take their chairs outside, turn them back to front, straddle them, and watch life as it goes by. The doggedness of these observers sometimes carries the hallmark of mad genius: sometimes they sit out there all their lives and see nothing but the face of the observer opposite. Then they die with a deep grudge against the world, convinced that it is a grey and boring place, because it rarely occurs to them to get up and go into the next street. Observers of life become restless in old age. They thrash about, glancing at their watches; it's one of those funny habits that old people have—a desire to protect time. At some point their voracity for life and for excitement grows stronger than that of a twenty-year-old. They talk a lot and they think a lot: their feelings are wild and vacuous all at once. Then they fizzle out quickly and quietly. As they die, they try to persuade everyone that they lived an expansive life. The impotent boast of their successes with women, the cowards of their heroism, the cretins of their wisdom.

Gienek—house painter and decorator by trade—had lived in the Marymont district for forty years, and had been observing local life for just as long. That Saturday

Gienek too was sitting outside in the garden, mindlessly gazing down the street. Now and then he spat and licked his parched lips; the declining day had been hot and oppressive. Gienek was irritated: nothing interesting had happened today, nobody had broken an arm, nobody had beaten anyone up, and Gienek was agonized by a sense of emptiness and boredom. He kicked a dog that got under his feet, and yawning gloomily, gazed at the street. It was deserted; rare passing cars raised clouds of heated sand. He had lost all hope of seeing a bit of life when he felt someone jostling his arm. He raised his sleepy eyes and saw his neighbour, Maliszewski.

'Come on,' said Maliszewski.

'Where?'

'Not far.'

'What for?'

'Wanna see something?' said Maliszewski.

He was a small man with a genial face and cunning little eyes. Despite a ponderous appearance, he could move as fast and nimbly as a young cat.

'What is it?' asked Gienek, and yawned, tired by the heat.

'A lad,' said Maliszewski.

'And so what?'

'A satyr,' said Maliszewski. 'He's with a girl. Now do you get it?'

'All right,' said Gienek. As he stood up, his heart was filled with hope. 'Is she pretty?' he asked excitedly.

'Young and pretty,' said Maliszewski. 'I'm telling you, there's a good job being done there.' Suddenly he grew impatient. 'Are you coming or not?' he asked.

'It's pointless,' said Gienek. 'They'll be over and done with it before we get there. It's pointless, I tell you.'

'They're not over fifty like you,' said Maliszewski. 'They can go on fooling around for ages. When I was young I could do it for hours, I sure could. We'll pick up my brother-in-law and go straight there, OK? He's just back from work and he'll be happy to join us. Oh, look, here he comes!'

Indeed, a stout young man was coming down the street. His shirt sleeves were rolled up, and he had a blade of grass in his mouth. His eyes were dozy and derisive, his eyelids heavy.

'Henio,' called Maliszewski, 'over here a moment!'

Henio came up and leaned against the fence. His brow was damp with sweat.

'Hi,' he said. 'How's it going, Gienek?'

'Henio,' said Maliszewski, 'come with us.'

'It's hot,' said Henio; he licked his lips and sighed. 'You can't breathe in this heat. A saint couldn't put up with it. Where do you wanna go?'

'I was up at the allotments,' said Maliszewski. 'I saw this lad with a girl.'

'A slut?' asked Henio. He spat out the blade of grass, then picked a new one and bit it hard.

'No way,' said Maliszewski. 'I'm telling you, she's young and pretty.'

'We can go along,' said Henio. 'You know me: I like to get a look at life. But if the girl's ugly, you're buying the drinks,' he said, addressing Maliszewski.

They set off and were soon among the allotment gardens. People came here after work to inspect their potatoes, tomatoes and carrots. But now it was deserted: the torpid, sultry day had exhausted everyone—people were sitting at home.

'It's so stuffy,' said Henio. 'I can't do nothing on a day like this. My head aches non-stop.'

'Those two must be feeling hot and all,' said Gienek.

'I bet they do,' said Maliszewski. 'We'll soon cool them down. Right, Henio?'

'Last year there was a bloke came here with a girl too,' said Henio. 'They kept coming all summer.'

'And?'

'That's all. I guess they just didn't have a flat.'

'Were they married?' asked Gienek with effort; he was dreaming of a glass of cold, tangy beer.

'I dunno. Maybe. She was nice-looking too.'

'A blonde?' asked Gienek, though he didn't really care; he was still feeling painful emptiness and distaste.

'A brunette,' said Henio. 'I remember her very well. The bloke had fair hair. I couldn't understand why such a dolly bird was going around with a creep.'

'Who knows,' muttered Gienek, spitting thick saliva. He was annoyed with Henio for reminding him that his own wife was ugly and rather stupid. 'She was probably just a slut,' he said.

'Maybe…Quiet now,' said Maliszewski. He walked in front, while the others slowly followed, trying not to make a noise. It was getting dark by now; the sun had fled, and bluish shadows lay on the grass. Finally Maliszewski turned around and called quietly: 'Come on!'

They tiptoed a few steps forwards, and saw a boy and girl, lying side by side. The girl was resting her head on the boy's arm, cuddling up to him the length of her body. There they lay, tired by love and heat, both young and good-looking—one dark, the other fair. The girl's dress was raised; she had long, sturdy brown legs.

'Pretty,' said Henio, 'very pretty.'

'I told you,' whispered Maliszewski.

They stood in silence; Gienek licked his lips again and thought of his wife with a shudder of disgust. Maliszewski smiled doltishly. Henio's heavy eyelids drooped even lower as he shifted from foot to foot. All of a sudden he asked testily: 'Are we gonna do something?'

'You do it,' said Maliszewski. 'Do something to them to make them hold their sides laughing for the rest of their lives. You can do it, Henio.'

'Hey, Henio,' said Gienek, 'better still, give them a fright. She's awful pretty,' he went on, snapping his fingers. 'I ain't seen a doll like that for ages. She's still a kid. They shouldn't be doing that.' Suddenly he lost patience. 'Do something to them, Henio, or I'll throw a bomb at them!'

'Hold on,' said Henio. 'Better let me do it.'

He gazed at the girl's brown thighs a while, his face the picture of torment. Then he emerged from behind the tree and stood before the young couple. He squinted at them and said: 'Playing at mummies and daddies, eh? Cheers!'

Maliszewski and Gienek burst out laughing. The boy leaped to his feet and stammered: 'What do you want?'

'Nothing,' said Henio very slowly. He stood facing the boy and swayed on his feet, still chewing his blade of grass and spitting green saliva. Then he said: 'Mind how you go, sonny. That's what I came to tell you. Always mind how you go.'

Maliszewski emerged from behind the tree and stood beside Henio.

'Very nice,' he said, looking at the girl with his little grey eyes. 'I could do with one like that. Perhaps we'll get to know each other, Miss.'

'Imbecile,' said the girl, standing behind the boy. She was red and flustered; Gienek watched as her slender shoulders trembled, and thought again of his ugly, fat, shapeless wife with disgust.

'Why, you slut!' said Maliszewski, his eyes bloodshot with rage. He spoke fast, as if choking: 'You're nothing but a common whore, get it? I've got a daughter older than you, you little tart.'

'Get out of here,' said the boy, looking them in the eyes beseechingly. 'Would you please get out of here. We haven't done you any harm. Please, I beg you.'

'Who are you begging, Janek?' said the girl. 'That old fool?'

'Shut your bird's trap,' said Henio, 'or I'll shut it for you. And don't you try acting the clown either. I'll shut her trap, I say.'

'Shut your own trap,' said the girl, casting him a look of contempt. She was frantically upset, but trying her best to laugh scornfully. 'You swine,' she said, and burst into tears.

'Hey,' said Henio, tugging her by the arm. 'Who are you calling names? You come here to do your whoring and you've still got the nerve to make remarks?'

The boy flinched, then he hit Henio in the face, once and again. It happened so fast that Henio only had time to blink. But the next second he grabbed the boy by the hair and smashed his face against his own knee. Then he punched him in the mouth and threw him to the ground.

'Is that enough, my good man?' he asked. 'If not, I can provide extra service. At a discount; there's a very nice graveyard here.' And he burst into a torrent of extremely filthy abuse. He closed his eyes, but he could still see the girl's long brown legs.

'Come on, Janek,' said the girl, wiping blood from the boy's face. 'We'll get even yet,' she said to them. And once they'd gone a few steps she shouted hysterically: 'You're old scum, not men!'

They went home. They walked back through the allotment gardens.

'It's close,' said Henio. 'It's probably gonna rain.' He sighed and said: 'That girl was really pretty. Why did you call her a whore? You don't know her. How could you tell?'

'I never said that,' said Maliszewski. 'You were the one who said it.'

'Me?'

'Yeah, you.'

'Don't take the piss. I've never seen her before.'

'I have,' said Maliszewski. 'It's not the first time they've been here. They're very much in love.'

'What'll happen now?' asked Gienek.

'I dunno. But I do know they're courting. And I know today was their first time together.'

'How do you know?' asked Gienek idly.

'I heard him asking her. He was afraid, and so was she. I heard them talking each other into it. They were scared of having a baby, that's what they said. But they were probably more scared of each other.'

'It's always like that the first time,' said Henio. 'I was scared too.'

'Everyone's scared of that the first time,' said Maliszewski. 'But why did you smack him?'

'That's what you wanted.'

'I didn't know it would come to that. He said such a strange thing to her...'

'What was it?'

'I can't remember.'

'It's clouding over,' said Gienek.

'That's it, he said something about clouds,' said Maliszewski. 'A poem. I tell you, they're in love.'

'They won't be making love now,' said Gienek. 'They'll have had enough of each other for good. After what's happened they won't stand the sight of each other. It's all come to nothing.'

'I know what it was,' said Maliszewski. 'I've remembered. He told her if they did it, it'd be their first step in the clouds. That's what he said, but it was in a poem. But all she said was: "I'm scared, I'm scared", and she cried.'

'Maybe she was scared of the pain?'

'I don't think so,' said Maliszewski. 'I don't think she was scared of the pain. That comes later on. Life, other people, gossip. But the first time it really is like being in the clouds. People in love can't see a thing.'

'Us too?' asked Henio.

'They won't be in love any more,' said Gienek. 'If something like that happened to me, I'd stop loving the girl.'

Suddenly he became dejected: emptiness was making him suffer again. They left the allotments and walked back down the street.

'No,' said Henio. 'They won't be in love any more. Something similar once happened to me too. And after it I stopped loving the girl.'

'Something like that has happened to all of us before now,' said Maliszewski. 'But why the hell did you smash him in the face?'

'He hit me first,' said Henio. 'Are we going for that beer?'

'Yes. I guess that girl won't come here again.'

'I guess not,' said Gienek. 'And why did you call her that name?'

'Someone once called my girl that,' said Maliszewski. 'And as God's my witness, I still don't know why.'

'And you stopped loving her after that?'

'No,' said Maliszewski. He paused, and then with sudden anger he said: 'Leave me alone, damn you! I don't believe in any kind of love. I don't trust my own woman either. I don't trust no one.'

'It's a silly business,' said Henio. 'It's clouding over,' he said, glancing at the sky. 'What was that he said?'

'I think it was a step into the rain or something,' said Maliszewski wearily. 'Let's get that beer ... Either rain or a storm…I can't remember. I don't wanna remember. If I hadn't remembered, there wouldn't have been all that fuss.'

'It'll rain tomorrow,' said Henio.

'It always rains on Sunday,' said Gienek, and scowled; once again he thought of his hideous wife, of the boy, of tomorrow, of the lovely girl, her long brown legs, her breasts, her fresh red lips, her strong, tanned nape and her green, terrified eyes, and as he had to say something once again he jabbered: 'It always rains on Sunday…'

The Palace of Culture (1957)

Kazimierz Orłoś

Our house is made of red bricks, planks and sheet metal. My father built it before he started drinking, and my grandpa helped him. Grandpa was younger then and didn't drink either. Now he sits on a bench by the pot-bellied stove all day and doesn't understand much of what we say to him. The roof of our house is made of wooden planks with sheets of metal on top. There are two rooms inside. One is a kitchen, where the stove is, but Mummy doesn't let us call that room the kitchen. We live there in the autumn, spring and winter. There's no pot-bellied stove in the other room, but it's bigger. We live there in the summer. We wash in a basin or by the well, and we go to the outhouse in the courtyard. And we have no electricity because they haven't connected us up yet. We burn paraffin lamps.

There are three of us: me, meaning Jola, my younger sister Małgosia, and Janek who's the youngest. We live with Mummy and Grandpa who doesn't understand much, as I've already said. Ever since he started drinking, Dad doesn't live with us any more. He moved in with Hela, the buffet lady. Mummy sometimes talks about our dad to Mrs Kowalczyk, who lives next door. When they talk about Hela, Mummy calls her 'that slut' or even worse—the W word.

Sometimes our father comes to visit. It's all right when he's not drunk, but if he's pickled there's always a row. Mummy refuses to let him in, and blocks the door with chairs, while our dad shouts and swears, and when he finally manages to get inside the house, he starts hitting her. Mummy calls for help and cries. Janek and Małgosia hide under the bed, and I run to find Mrs Kowalczyk. Her husband comes to calm our dad down but the row is usually over by then. Mummy cries, and our father goes to sleep on the bed, with Małgosia and Janek still sitting under it. Finally Dad wakes up and leaves, but Mummy's upset for the rest of the day.

Worst of all is in the winter. We burn sticks and pinecones that we've collected in the summer, and our coal ration, but there's never enough. When the stove gets red hot we're warm, but once it cools down we're freezing. The wind forces its way into our kitchen through the leaky walls. When the temperature falls below zero, the little panes of glass in the windows get covered in white frost. When the snow falls on our house, next morning we have to dig paths to the outhouse and the well. At night we huddle under the quilt and under Mummy's coat. We can hear the wind wailing and Grandpa snoring. Sometimes it's so cold we can't get to sleep, then Janek starts crying, Mummy wakes up and comforts him, and Grandpa starts to curse, but we don't know if he does it in his sleep or for real.

In spring and summer it's better. We live on the edge of the woods, which start just behind our house. There are lots of cottages like ours here—either made of stone or wood, better or worse. They're all at the edge of the woods, along the road to the city. Horse-drawn carts go up and down the road, because everyone here has horses, now and then cars go by, and one red-and-white bus, with the biggest cloud of dust behind it, if the weather's dry. From here you can hardly see the city, just the church towers and the Palace of Culture. Most often we look at the Palace of Culture. The sun reflects off the golden spire, and we can even see the white stone walls. They look nice against the blue sky.

Janek in particular likes to look at the Palace. Holding a slice of bread sprinkled with sugar, grimy, in his drooping underpants held up by braces, he stands there and stares at it for hours. The only thing he finds more interesting is Józek's doves. Józek is Mrs Kowalczyk's son. He's got a dovecote, next door to us, on the roof of the shed. He often lets the doves out to fly around. They're white, he only has two brown ones. Janek stands beside Józek and tilts his head to watch them flying. They turn circles in a flock above the roofs, either high or low above us. We squint, because the sunlight bounces off the doves' white wings. Once they've all come down again and are perched on the roof of the shed, Józek lures them under a net. First he scatters some buckwheat. Then he pulls on a string and lowers a flap. The doves are trapped. Only then does Janek return to looking at the Palace.

Sometimes we play till late in the yard or in the woods, until Mummy calls us in for supper. We usually have potato soup or potatoes with sour milk, and a piece of bread and margarine. Mummy earns little and works hard. She travels into the city and cleans the rooms, halls and corridors in offices there. She works from six a.m. to five p.m. On the first of each month she gets five hundred zlotys, and that's a very happy day. Mummy brings us half a kilo of sweets and does the shopping. We wait for her outside the house. Janek gets a handful of sweets and Grandpa gets a small bottle of vodka. Then Mummy divides up the money for the whole month and starts to feel sad because she knows there won't be enough until the first of the month comes around again. She puts the money away under the straw mattress.

Every morning, if it's the school year, I go to school at eight. Before that, I give Małgosia, Janek and Grandpa their breakfast—porridge and bread. They stay at home alone, though sometimes Mrs Kowalczyk looks in to check what's happening—if Małgosia and Janek are playing outside and if Grandpa is dozing on the bench. Anyway, what danger could they be in until I get back? No one's going to come here and rob them. What on earth would they take? Perhaps the money Mummy hides under the straw mattress. But how would they know where it is?

As I've already said, in the summer we play outside. Sometimes we run around the woods with the neighbours' kids. Then we gaze at the golden spire of the Palace of Culture again, or at Józek's doves. Mummy calls us in for lunch or supper, we have our soup and go outside again. Nothing has changed for as long as I can remember. I'm ten years old, Małgosia's six, and Janek is four.

Sometimes Janek gets sick. He was ill for three weeks recently, so Mummy had to summon a doctor from the District Council health centre. He was due to come by bus at three p.m. Małgosia and I went to the stop to show him the way, so he wouldn't get lost among all the small houses on our estate. Earlier Mummy had swept the floor, wiped the window panes and smoothed the blankets on the beds. She took the day off from her cleaning job in the city. She dressed Janek in a clean shirt, and took Grandpa outside to sit in front of the house.

It's warm now, it's spring, and the fruit trees are blossoming around the houses. We just have the one apple tree. It has blossomed too, and its flowery branches look into the kitchen window. When we went to fetch the doctor, there was a scent of those flowers everywhere, and the air was all spring-like and transparent, so you could see the Palace of Culture well. The golden spire was shining in the sunlight. I told Małgosia we'd take Janek to the city to see the Palace close up, because then he'd be sure to get well more quickly.

When the doctor came we immediately recognized him. On the way to our house he asked us our names, if we both go to school and if we have dolls. When I said we don't have any, he was very surprised. Then he examined Janek, while we watched through the window, from the yard, because Mummy told us to go out. Janek was sitting up in bed, all skinny and tiny, without his shirt, which he must have taken off. The doctor tapped on his back, put a teaspoon into his mouth and looked down his throat, and finally listened through a tube to his little heart beating. Then he spent ages writing something on some bits of paper and talked to Mummy. Before leaving he stroked

Janek on the head too, and outside he shook hands with Grandpa, and Grandpa was very pleased.

We took the doctor back to the bus stop, and when we got home, Janek was sitting up in bed, crying, and Mummy was at the table, looking sad. She said our brother was very sick, so she'd have to buy medicine, but then there wouldn't be enough money to live on. I asked if we could show Janek the Palace of Culture, because it was so clearly visible and the spire was shining nicely in the sun. At first Mummy refused to let us, but we begged her, and Janek joined in, insisting he wanted to see it, and I said that if he did, it would help him and he'd get better sooner. Finally Mummy agreed, so we wrapped our little brother in a blanket, then I picked him up and carried him outside. We stood under the apple tree, from where you get the best view, so Janek could admire the Palace in the sunshine, and especially the golden spire.

'Oh!' he said. 'Oh!' He pointed at the Palace and asked: 'So what does it have inside?'

Małgosia and I didn't know, it was only once we'd carried Janek back inside that Mummy told us everything.

'Inside there are great big halls, corridors, lifts, red carpets that you walk on and lots of people. And there are crystal chandeliers sparkling overhead.'

'What are lifts?' asked Janek. 'And what are chandeliers?'

'Lifts,' said Mummy, 'are like little rooms in which you can ride up to any floor you wish, and chandeliers are like enormous lamps. Big enough on purpose to light up the biggest halls. Altogether the Palace is enormous. It has a hundred floors and a hundred halls, and at the top there are balconies and terraces from where you can see the whole city, and our house too. Who knows, perhaps you can even see the mountains from one side and the sea from the other.'

'And who lives in the Palace?' asked Janek.

'Nobody lives there. There are all sorts of offices inside it. The people just come in the morning to work, or to view the city from the top floor. Nobody's there at night.'

'So we couldn't go and live there either?'

'No, we couldn't. But wait a while, when you get better we'll go to the city so you can see the Palace for yourself. Just you get better, please.'

* * *

Our brother was sick for three weeks. Sometimes he was better, sometimes worse. His fever would suddenly return, and then he'd cough and cry. There were moments when we thought he was going to die, and what sort of a life would we have without Janek? But luckily he didn't die, and something that definitely helped him was me and Mummy telling him about the Palace of Culture. He couldn't wait for the day when we'd go to the city and he'd see it all with his own eyes.

And then finally the day came when Janek was well again. It was summer, and as in the past we could play outside, run to the woods and watch Józek's doves flying. Grandpa sat on the little bench as usual, talking to himself or to someone only he could see. Mummy would come home, we'd have our potato soup, and in the evening we'd go to bed. Until one Sunday we went to the city.

The bus was jam-packed, and although we wanted to look out of the window we couldn't see a thing. Then the tram was crowded too, and Mummy accidentally trod on a lady's foot, and that lady began to shout at her to look out, and said perhaps she'd never been on a tram before. And Mummy told the lady that she was probably the one who'd never been on a tram before, because she ought to know that when it's crowded, people might tread on each other's feet. And they went on shouting at each other like that until Janek started to cry. Luckily we'd reached the stop where we were getting off. And when we did, we saw the Palace of Culture close up. There it stood before us, all lit up by the sun, so bright and so big that it seemed to go right up to the sky. As we walked slowly across a huge square the Palace got nearer and nearer, and now and then high up a window flashed as the sun bounced off it. And as we were walking along like that, Janek said the Palace was so huge that all the people could live in it. Then Mummy and I laughed a lot at Janek, only Małgosia didn't, because she was thinking the same thing.

And finally, once we were very close, the Palace shielded the sky, and we walked in its shadow all the way to the huge steps up which you had to enter through a large gateway. And continuing on our way, we passed some enormous figures, holding hammers and spades, as if standing on guard for the Palace. They were great big people made of stone, standing next to stone columns and just staring with those bulging eyes of theirs at the square we'd crossed. Janek was speechless with amazement, gazing all around him, while Mummy held his hand tight so he wouldn't get lost.

The large hall that we entered was crowded with a huge number of people going in and out of the Palace, and there overhead hung the vast crystal chandeliers Mummy had told us about. On we went, to yet more stairs, across a floor that shone like everything here, into a hall where there were lifts, just as she had told us, so we could go up in the lift to the very top. But just then a fat gentleman in a blue uniform with gold buttons and a blue cap with a black peak blocked our way, and asked where we were going. Mummy said we wanted to take the lift to the top floor, to see the view of the city, and maybe we'd see our house beyond the city too. But the gentleman went on blocking our way and asked if we were with a tour group or on our own. And when Mummy said we were on our own, he asked if we had tickets. But we didn't have any tickets, and anyway Mummy hadn't brought any money for tickets, so she started asking the man to let us in. She said we'd only go up for a few minutes and we'd be straight back down. But he said that was impossible, because without tickets he couldn't let us in.

We stood there for quite a while, listening to Mummy as she begged the man, and the whole time people with tickets or with tour groups kept going past, staring at us. And he let them all through, it was only us he refused to let in. I remember Mummy saying: 'Please have pity! I just want to show the kids the view of the city.' And the guard replying: 'I can't help you. Those are the rules. Please buy some tickets.' And he got louder and louder: 'Please buy some tickets!'

And I also remember the way he pushed us back when Mummy pushed us forwards, and blocked our path with his outspread hands. Until Mummy realized he would never let us in, so finally she said in a loud voice: 'The Palace is for the people, not the people for the Palace! You don't understand that.'

And then he started shouting.

'Please go away, please go away or I'll call the security guards!'

At that point Mummy grabbed Janek and Małgosia by the hands and quickly began to walk away, while I ran after them. First we went down the shining stairs, we almost ran across the hall beneath the crystal chandeliers to the huge gates and on, down the stone steps and into the square. We passed the columns and stone figures again, first in the shadow of the Palace, and then in the sunlight, all the way back to the tram. Mummy didn't say a word, but I could see how badly upset she was. She didn't even answer Janek's question about why that man had refused to let us in.

We went back in the tram, and then the bus again. On the way home the crowd wasn't as bad, so we could sit by the window and gaze at the Palace from afar. And once we were walking down the road from the bus stop, we saw our wooden house in the distance, and close up Grandpa on the threshold, saying something to himself, spreading his hands and shrugging.

The Presence
(2007)

Hanna Krall

1

The former residents left behind a mirabelle plum tree, some glass beads, and some ghosts.

These were the residents of the apartment houses and courtyards on Wałowa, Franciszkańska and Nalewki (now Anders) Streets.

2

The mirabelle plum tree tried to get away. It leaned over and stretched its branches ahead of itself. In preparation for the journey, it pulled its roots from the ground. The new residents surrounded its trunk with a steel band and secured it with ropes. The plum tree stopped in mid-move. The women made jam out of its slightly sour yellow fruits.

3

The beads were lying near the tree, trodden into the ground. They were small and round, in vivid, cheerful colours. The new residents' children washed them in sieves and strung them on threads; nylon fishing line wasn't a familiar item then. All the little girls in the neighbourhood wore those colourful glass necklaces.

4

The beads may have been left behind by a lampshade manufacturer. He may have used them for fringes or for sewn-on decoration.

In the list of pre-war Warsaw firms there was no lampshade maker in the vicinity.

They may have been left behind by a manufacturer of something called 'jet products'.

There was one, but some distance away, on Nowolipie Street.

Embroiderers?

There were two, close by, on Wałowa Street. But why would they need that many beads for embroidery?

Carnival items?

Feathers and artificial flowers?

Costume jewellery?

There was a jeweller on the list of firms. J. Alfus, 24 Nalewki Street.

On an old map of the city that includes the house numbers, number 24 is on the corner of Franciszkańska Street, and has two entrances, from both streets.

So it's right here.

Joyful, not to say exciting news.

Why exactly?

Why should one be excited by the information that someone named J. Alfus left a supply of beads behind in a courtyard on Franciszkańska Street?

He was probably preparing for the approaching season. For the carnival of 1940.

In my imagination, Mrs Alfus said:

'I was always in favour of something practical. Winter boots...Pickled cabbage...Who needs your glass beads during a war?'

'The war won't last forever,' Mr Alfus consoled his wife and himself.

(Maybe I'm wrong, and he was the one who wanted something practical, while she was attracted to gaiety and finery. And it was Mrs Alfus who assured her husband that one day there would be a carnival again.)

We don't know Mr and Mrs A.'s first names, but we do know their phone number:

11 17 29

The modern payphone tells one to add the figure 8.

A firm named Alu answers. It sounds like an abbreviation of the surname of the former owners. The firm called Alu has nothing to do with glass beads. It uses glass, but for windows and doors. The glass is burglar-proof.

The sense of excitement is gone.

5

The ghosts had taken a liking to the new residents on Anders Street, a not-so-young couple, who worked as a seamstress and a market trader. Their block was built after the war on the rubble of the apartment house on the corner.

They had been feeling someone's presence for a couple of years.

It wasn't a hostile presence. Someone would knock at the door. Tip the lid off something in the empty kitchen. Stride across the floor. Stroke the cat. The cat would sniff them, purr, and present its head to be stroked. They thought it could see a child, but the cat would jump onto the table, stretch its neck and stare. There was someone tall in front of it. Not a child, no. Someone tall... Sometimes a whole crowd came to visit. There'd be a feeling of commotion, hustle and bustle. They had the sensation of being surrounded by a silent, mute hum.

They thought they were being visited by their own family spirits. Their Ukrainian brother-in-law, for instance, who'd been a bundle of nerves.

They set up his picture and lit a ritual candle. They were told that if the flame flickered, wavered or waned it meant the brother-in-law bore a grudge or had unfinished business in this world.

The candle burned steadily, so they thought: not the Ukrainian brother-in-law. Maybe it was one of their mothers? Or a brother?

Once again, they set up pictures and lit candles. They watched them closely all night. The flame was even quieter than for the brother-in-law.

They went to see the priest. He didn't know whose souls were wandering around their house but he prayed, recited something in Latin and sprinkled holy water in every corner.

The saucepans went on rattling just as before, and the cat went on greeting the invisible guests.

They asked Jude for help, the patron saint of hopeless causes.

They approached an exorcist.

'In your house,' she wrote, 'there are five Household Spirits and eighteen Accompanying Spirits. I'll soon send them off to another level of existence.'

The exorcist failed to send the spirits off to another level. They preferred their current level, on Anders Street.

6

The wife was first to hit upon the idea that the ghosts were Jewish. In the past, no one but Jews lived in the entire neighbourhood, and during the war the ghetto was here.

'I think you're right,' agreed the husband.

'My father had a clothes stall on Kercel Square,' added the wife, 'and he knew a lot of Jews in person.'

'Sure,' agreed the husband, 'there were a hell of a lot of Yids around here.'

'What a way to speak!' said the wife indignantly.

'I don't mean it nastily,' explained the husband, 'but those are the facts.'

7

Bad luck began to plague them.

They took clothing from the wholesaler's to the suburban bazaars but people stopped buying it.

They took cappuccino coffee. People stopped buying that too.

They made warm hoods, but there was no cold weather.

They made ladies' skirts. The owner of a boutique ordered a batch of skirts patterned with large, golden-yellow sunflowers. The British queen wore sunflowers on a navy-blue background during her visit to Poland, so it was the trendiest design at all the bazaars.

'You sew well,' the boutique owner praised them, 'but why doesn't anyone want to buy your things?'

They placed an advertisement in the paper. An entrepreneur in urgent need of outworkers replied. He promised to come by. He didn't turn up. A month later his wife called: 'He had a car crash on his way to see you.'

They realized their bad luck was connected with the Jewish ghosts and invited a rabbi to their home.

8

'My grandmother was born in Baligród,' began the rabbi. 'She knew Warsaw. From her stories I've never forgotten the word Nalewki. The only Polish word I knew on arriving in Warsaw: Na-lew-ki.'

'That's here,' said the householders animatedly, and showed him the street out of the window. 'In your grandmother's day it was Nalewki Steet. In the communist era it was Nowotka Street. Under democracy it's Anders Street. So what do the Jewish ghosts want from us, please, Rabbi? We don't wish them any harm.'

'I'm not surprised you can feel a Jewish presence,' said the rabbi. 'I'd be surprised if anyone can't feel it.'

'I've always been concerned about their fate,' sighed the housewife. 'Only yesterday, in a TV series, a Jew brought his granddaughter out of the ghetto and asked people to hide her. It was enough to make me weep. Then he ordered pork knuckle at a bar, swallowed some arsenic and drank beer. I cried, didn't I?' she said, addressing her husband.

'And then what?' asked the rabbi, interested. 'Does the granddaughter survive?'

'Yes, she does. The series has been on before, and she survived, so there'll be a happy ending this time too.'

'And what do the Jewish spirits want from us, Rabbi?'

'I don't know,' admitted the rabbi. 'In normal times the soul goes off to heaven, but the war was not a normal time.'

'There was fighting here. The remains weren't buried. Do the souls of people who haven't been buried go off to heaven too?'

'I don't know,' said the rabbi.

'Maybe the unburied souls roam the world…'

'I don't know.'

'So what can you do for us, Rabbi?'

'Pray. That's all I can do.'

He took out a prayer book and recited a psalm in Hebrew.

The one about the Shepherd, by whose side we lack nothing. Who feeds us in green pastures and comforts us beside still waters. With whom we are not afraid in the dark valley of death. Whose shepherd's staff guides us. In whose house we shall live for ever . . .

9

Josek Braun?

Just like the housewife's father he traded on Kercel Square. The housewife's father sold clothes, and Josek Braun sold haberdashery items.

He was small and stocky, said Jasia Jochwed, Josek's daughter. But Mietek, her father's brother, was tall. Before the war he had a stall on Kercel Square too, and in the ghetto he worked for the Funeral Society.

If the new residents' cat jumps up on the table because it can see someone tall, perhaps it's the neighbour from Kercel Square, Mietek Braun.

What about Dorka's relatives?

She had parents, grandparents, uncles, in-laws, brothers and cousins—all from here, from Wałowa Street. And they were all quite tall.

'Is that possible, Dorka?'

'Yes, it is, they were quite tall.'

Jakub, Dorka's father, was quite tall.

His brother Icek was quite tall.

Her uncles Szlojme and Chaim, her mother's brothers, were quite tall.

The husbands of her aunts, her mother's sisters—Aunt Hinda and Aunt Rajzł, and Aunt Roza, and Aunt Pesia— were all quite tall.

But the tallest was Lajbl, Fela's husband. And he was distinguished and handsome too. And rich.

Fela, one of Dorka's sisters, married him during the war and they lived on Wałowa Street too. Fela was in the bunker but she said she didn't want to carry on. She didn't want the bunker, the darkness and the fear, she said, and went on her way.

Where did she go?

And where did they all go?

10

A sepia photograph (one last photograph): the family on the Feast of Purim. The women are in Sabbath dresses. Dorka can remember the original colours and even the fabrics and cut. Her mother: a black velvet dress, buttoned like an overcoat, with a gold trim. Aunt Roza: also black, but with embroidery. Aunt Pesia: silk, brown. Aunt Mania: navy blue with a white zip. She remembered the hairstyles, those elaborate rollers, tightly curled underneath or on top. With the exception of Aunt Brońcia, who didn't have curls, but wore her hair in a bun. The serious girl next to her is her daughter, a law student. Each of them have children beside them; next to Aunt Pesia is her older son, who was soon to have his Bar Mitzvah, and the younger one wasn't in the photograph. 'He must have stayed at home and was asleep,' guessed Dorka.

And this entire company—in a modest, modern flat on Anders Street! No wonder there was commotion, hustle and bustle.

The same Sabbath dresses that never had time to wear out. The hair in curls and in a bun that never went grey. Only the children had changed. Aunt Pesia's sons had grown up—both the older one, who had his Bar Mitzvah in the ghetto, and the younger one, who wasn't in the picture because he had stayed at home and slept. They had had time to grow up, because between the Feast of Purim and Treblinka three years went by.

Between the Feast of Purim and the visit to Anders Street three years went by.

And Mietek Braun, the neighbour from Kercel Square, could have been there too, with his father and brother . . .

And Mr and Mrs Alfus, who wouldn't have had to come from anywhere because they were at home, on the spot. Mrs Alfus would have put on a necklace made of beads that nobody needed in the ghetto. Of round, glass beads, as red as blood, as wine, or as rowanberries.

11

They only feel safe in memory. Released from the bunkers, the darkness and fear. Carefree. Chatty. Distinguished and tall. Their death was a privilege. After no other death would they be as distinguished, tall, rich and beautiful.

12

The rabbi sang the prayer *El malei rachamim*.

'Merciful God, provide a sure rest beneath Thy wings for the souls of…'

He paused, because after these words one should say the names of the dead.

'I'll say the street names,' he suggested. 'Dictate them to me.'

'Provide a sure rest beneath Thy wings for the souls of the residents of…'

'Franciszkańska, Wałowa and Nalewki Streets,' prompted the householders, as if they were the rabbi's altar boys.

The sonorous, plaintive, Jewish singing echoed throughout the flat. All the neighbours could hear it. They must have thought there was something about Jews on TV again. But it was simply the New York grandson of Tauba Roth, who grew up in Baligród, praying for the former residents of Franciszkańska, Wałowa and Nalewki Streets.

The View from Above and Below (2011)

Antoni Libera

For Janusz Szuber

I

The window of his bedroom in their spacious flat on the
third floor of the corner house at number 8, Szpitalna
Street, looked north, onto Hortensja Street. The main
thing he could see from it was the huge square block of the
Main Post Office, which had its entrance on Napoleon
Square, and beyond that, protruding above the rooftops,
the twin spires of Holy Cross Church on Krakowskie
Przedmieście; further off, slightly to the left, was the bright
blue, heavily patinated cupola of the Lutheran church,
topped with a round turret. Every Sunday afternoon his

parents took him there for the service, and one day, in the building next door to it, he would attend the Mikołaj Rej Academy for Boys, run by the Parish of the Holy Trinity since the start of the century.

But for now he was only nine years old, went to the primary school on Traugutt Street, and had plenty of time to himself. Entirely given over to his job at the conservatory, his father was away from home for days at a time. His mother often went abroad, to Vienna or to Italy, and then he was cared for by Honorata, the maid, who occupied the servant's room; now and then his father's younger brother Oskar would look after him, an architect and urban planner.

It was the second half of August, 1929.

He had spent the holidays on the coast in Zoppot, as usual, with his mother and father and their friends, Mr and Mrs Kuryłło, who had a son slightly older than he was. It was comfortable there, and boring. But now, faced with long, hot, idle hours alone within the stone walls of the capital, despite its monotony, that recent time seemed interesting.

He looked down at the streets. Hortensja Street, then Przeskok, Warecka, and beyond that Świętokrzyska. He knew this area like the back of his hand. Quite early on his parents had let him go out on his own to fetch the newspapers or to post a letter. He often prolonged these errands to get his fill of freedom. The streets had a different flavour when he was alone compared with walking down them in the company of the adults. Even within a radius of one hundred metres from his home he felt a tremor of emotion— as if he were far away from it, out on the open sea, not entirely sure of making it back to base. Would he be able to get home alone if he were suddenly kidnapped, carried off to a district he'd only ever heard about, such as Wola or Ochota, and left there, in a completely unfamiliar place? He should be able to manage. After all, he knew he lived in the centre, right by the Main Post Office, in between Marszałkowska Street and Nowy Świat Street, which ran parallel to it. Everyone knew these places and anyone could tell him which way to go. And yet he was never rid of a touch of anxiety, fuelled by memories of his few trips out of the city by car, when he'd gazed through the window at the distant suburbs or the streets of the Praga district, which were like another world entirely. Oh, he wouldn't want to live there, and especially end up there alone! Those places were alien, dangerous, threatening and predatory. He doubted he'd ever get home from there.

The doorbell rang. That was odd—at this time of day? It was around noon. The dairymaid, or the postman, bringing a registered letter, came much earlier. He jumped off his stool by the window, went to the sitting-room door, and kept still to listen. He heard Honorata go and ask:

'Who's there?', then the clank of the bolt and the resonant voice of Uncle Oskar.

He was pleased. He liked him. Uncle Oskar was lively, funny, and direct in his manner. He brought an entirely different spirit into their caustic, taciturn family. Cheerful, eloquent, enterprising and practical, he was passionate about sport, motorization and technology. He was keen on progress and took a hopeful view of the future. His older brother sneeringly called him a childish utopian; he by contrast saw the world in shades of black. But Uncle Oskar's most important character trait was his direct, relaxed approach to children: the fact that he showed genuine interest in them, talked to them as equals and was willing to play with them. He had none of his own yet, and wasn't even married.

'Such lovely weather,' he called at once from the threshold, 'and here you are, vegetating indoors! Put on your shoes and we'll be off. I'm taking you on a trip into the unknown.'

They trotted down the steps, then along Zgoda Street to reach Marszałkowska. There they boarded the number fourteen tram which ran towards Gdańsk Station.

Uncle Oskar's mouth was never shut.

'You're going to see something I'm sure you've never seen before. In fact it's rarely seen by anyone at all. Of course, one does see the construction site for a villa or a house, or the reshaping of a piece of land. But of an entire district? From nothing, from scratch? Perhaps once upon a time, long ago, when the city was first founded or when it was converted. When at the king's or the sovereign's command entire quarters were demolished to make way for a large edifice in his honour and glory. Like Florence Cathedral, or the Paris boulevards. But in the modern day? Maybe in America! In America, and here, in our city! Perhaps you've heard of Gdynia, and of Mr Kwiatkowski, the engineer...'

'Of course I have,' he replied smartly. 'I've even been to the port there. But where are we going?'

'You'll see. Beyond Gdańsk Station. Onto the grounds of a large construction site.'

Beyond the tram loop at Gdańsk Station, where formerly the line had ended and almost all the passengers got off, with rasping wheels the tram turned sharply to the right, drove onto a new track and accelerated on a downward slope. The district they were passing became wilder; on the left, stopped at a semaphore, was a panting locomotive, and on the right some undergrowth—it was sleepy, empty and uninhabited. Only once they had they gone through a gloomy, narrow tunnel to the other side of the train tracks did Uncle Oskar come back to life and start holding forth again.

'Look over there, at the stone walls, those fortifications,' he said, pointing to the right, as the tram climbed Krajewski

Street. 'Do you know what that is? The Citadel. A damnable Russian bastion that stopped the city from developing for almost a hundred years. A punishment inflicted by tsar Nicholas the First in revenge for the bid for freedom known as the November Uprising. To keep us in his grip and nip rebellion in the bud. And impoverish the city in the process—both financially, because it was all built at the citizens' cost... do you know how much was spent on it? Eight and a half tons of gold! And in terms of urban planning too, because thousands and thousands of people were evicted from the site and their houses were demolished, after which any form of expansion was prohibited. Do you think there were just open fields around here? There were already some buildings here, the embryos of new districts. All that was razed to the ground. To "widen the approaches", to put up forts with Russian names. Nigh on a hundred years, a whole century of that subjugation! But finally the Germans chased them out of here. I remember it well, I'd just taken my school certificate exams. And none of those safeguards did them any good at all! They even destroyed them themselves during the evacuation. That was typical of them! To conquer, ruin, tyrannize, erect insane fortresses that serve no purpose other than to torment people, and then burn it all down and run off in a panic.'

The ground they were travelling across, though mostly full of nothing but excavations, looked extraordinary. Like in a fantastical painting. An abandoned world, solitary buildings standing alone in a field and just one moving point: their little red tramcar gliding slowly down the tracks. A sleepy, defunct world. Defunct? Or not yet born?

'We're building a new city here,' said Uncle Oskar, standing on the rear platform. 'From scratch, from nothing. That hasn't been done before. Cities used to grow gradually, spontaneously. Building after building, street after street. Now we're in a different age. Just imagine: you've got a piece of ground roughly 150 hectares in size and you're to settle a few thousand people on it from various professional groups. You're to build a small town. Parcel out the land, map the streets, intersections and squares. Take all the needs into consideration: supplies, schools, transport, a church. Plan it all out. We've already done that. It took a couple of years. Now we're putting it into life.'

The tram stopped suddenly and the last passenger apart from them got out. They were left alone in the tramcar.

'Invalids Square,' said Uncle Oskar with a sweeping gesture as they approached an imposing four-storey building. Painted white, it was dazzlingly bright in the strong August sun. The ground to the right of it had been excavated, and beyond it some barracks and low-rise houses were under construction. 'Just like in Paris! They've got a Place des Invalides there too. Vast, colossal. They're going to hold major military parades here. Polish Army Avenue will be eighty metres wide, and a long way over there, on the left, it'll be topped by Grunwald Square.'

As he leaned over the railing on the rear platform of the tramcar gazing at it all, he felt as if he were riding on a narrow-gauge railway through wild, not urban terrain. It was an odd sensation. The clatter of the wheels, the new tracks, and wilderness surrounding them, a wasteland, just the occasional cottage and some scaffolding. All that was missing was a railway halt and a level-crossing attendant's booth.

'We're almost there,' said Uncle Oskar as a building rose before them, the front of which looked like a ship with no prow. 'We're entering Wilson Square, the *future* Wilson Square. For now it's just chaos, but I can see the shape of it already, because I drew it myself. A huge intersection: north-south, east-west, and a tram hub.'

Past the white ship-house the tramcar turned left and stopped behind it. 'Wilson Square, Ustronie Street!' cried the tram driver, then rotated the crank, which rattled pleasantly.

'And now watch out, we're approaching our destination,' said Uncle Oskar, putting a hand over his nephew's eyes before they alighted. He only removed it once they were on the ground, with their backs to the house resembling a ship.

Before them stretched a plot of land the size of a large playing field, about two metres below street level. Empty, compacted ground, with just a bit of faded grass growing here and there along the edges. Beyond it, on the far side they could see gravel, and further off in the distance a truly incredible sight. Standing in front of a massive building with an arched roof, like a factory hall or an aircraft hangar, there sprang up a huge brick chimney, twined with the spiral of a narrow iron staircase, and crowned with a circular gallery. In its turn it resembled a shapely lighthouse, but with no floodlight at the top. From a distance all this looked like an enormous steam engine that had been towed in here somehow, becoming bogged down in the mud and stuck for good.

'The boiler house, the heart of the housing estate,' Uncle Oskar proudly explained. 'That's how we build these days! No more coal-fired stoves, no more smoke and soot. Central heating! For several dozen buildings over the range of a kilometre! Now we're going to fit out the terrain with pipes, sewers and cables. The real construction will only start once this underground system of arteries is in place.'

They headed towards the chimney by running down a slope onto the flat plain of the construction site.

'An area for fêtes and entertainments, and in winter a skating rink,' explained Uncle Oskar. 'We've thought of everything. As in the perfect city.'

On the opposite side, beyond the strip of gravel, there was no more road. There were some long planks lying on the ploughed-up, muddy ground that served as a boardwalk. Finally they made their way to the foot of the chimney.

A moustachioed man in dark overalls emerged from the boiler house.

'Good day to you, Mr Engineer,' he said, greeting Uncle Oskar effusively. 'What brings you here at this time of day?'

'Nothing in particular,' said Uncle Oskar with a shrug. 'The sunshine, the good weather, the visibility. And the fact that I want to show this young fellow, who happens to be my nephew, what's going on around here. How a housing estate comes to life, how a new district is born.'

'A capital idea!' exclaimed the man in overalls, then he opened the gate into the spiral staircase. 'But slowly, very slowly,' he advised as they entered, 'because it makes you dizzy. You're not afraid of heights, are you, son?'

'On the contrary, he adores them,' Uncle Oskar replied for him. 'He'd love to spend all day sitting in the window, staring at the city from on high.'

They climbed the stairs, he in front and Uncle Oskar behind him, stopping every few steps. There were so many fascinating things to see! Above all, the view itself—stretching further and further and from an ever higher perspective, and on top of that the staircase, twisting like bindweed around the tapering circumference of the brick chimney. How was it attached? Straightaway, during construction, or only once it was finished? Did they have to put up scaffolding again for this purpose? And especially how had they given it such a harmonious shape? Two full rings and one half. He knew that everything was drawn out on a design and it looked nice. But what happened in reality? And anyway, how did they know what height the chimney should be in metres and how much to taper it? Was each layer of bricks narrower than the one before, or only some of them? How was it all calculated? How did they lay the bricks to make them fit together so tightly side by side, and yet turn a spiral? So many questions!

At last they reached the top. There was a faint breeze blowing. The circular gallery with a metal rail felt bouncy, and even seemed to sway a bit.

He didn't know which way to look. All around the view was similar, but slightly different. The immediate vicinity was full of construction mess: excavations, concrete casings and slabs, large cable reels, stacks of bricks and planks piled under a shelter, from which some narrow trolley-car tracks emerged. Further off there were a few buildings standing on their own, some already finished, even plastered, others still under construction. Like islands or oases on a wild plain. And beyond that, wreathed in pale blue mist, was the outline of a promenade, some dense under-growth and some trees, or the banks of the river Vistula.

There was total silence, just the occasional murmur of the wind or the sound of metallic knocking coming from below. He ran his eyes along the route of their walk from the tram stop, then directed his gaze along the tram rails. Until finally, far off in the distance he spied a little red dot, gliding at snail's pace towards Gdańsk Station.

'Well, have you had a good enough look yet?' asked Uncle Oskar at last. 'Now I'll show you what's going to be where. Let's start with the south, from Invalids Square. Over there, around the Citadel, a housing estate for the officer corps is already being built. Country house architecture: rows of small houses topped with clay roof tiles. And over there, to the west, down the long strip that's going to be Polish Army Avenue, they're building an estate for civil servants. Large, graceful, multistorey buildings, with garden squares in between them. And to the east, towards the river, there'll be what we're calling a journalist's estate, for private professionals. Similar in scale and character to the military one, but in a completely different style. Geometrical, angular. And here, around us,' said Uncle Oskar, pointing downwards and making a semi-circular gesture, 'there'll be a worker's estate: about ten blocks, with yards, a nursery school and a public library. The Warsaw Housing Cooperative, modernist in style.

And the whole thing forms a trapezium with its base facing east. Rather in response to the Citadel, which was also built in the shape of that figure. A city to spite a fortress. A modern district after a hundred years of blockade. With Wilson Square at its centre. Żoliborz—from the French, *joli bord*, pretty riverbank.'

At last Uncle Oskar fell silent and stared into the distance. As if he could see everything he'd been talking about with such ardour and expertise.

II

For some time, about six months, that outing with Uncle Oskar to Żoliborz under construction, and especially the sweeping view from the top of the boiler-house chimney filled his thoughts. During the long, boring hours he kept thinking about all sorts of details, imagining how the entire district would change over time. How the houses being built would block the scene, how the mapped-out streets would become a labyrinth and how gradually the ground would disappear beneath cobblestones or under lawns. How long might it take? Three years? Four? Longer? Or perhaps the work would only be finished in ten years' time, when he took his school certificate exams? He decided to have a chat with his uncle about it before long, and to ask him to take him there regularly, because he'd like to follow the progress of the work as it happened, and see how the ground was changing. So at the first opportunity he broached the topic, and of course his uncle agreed, announcing that in future they would go there by car, because he was planning to buy a used Fiat. But nothing came of it. Not because in the end his uncle hadn't bought a car, or had failed to keep his promise, but simply because in the course of time he himself had lost interest. All sorts of new experiences, at school and outside it, pushed the short, curious adventure from his mind. Elements of it did in fact come back to him now and then—images, snatches of remarks, and the general atmosphere—but ever less often, increasingly feebly, no longer stirring the same excitement. Finally he forgot the whole thing so much that when a few years later, a pupil at the academy by now, he travelled out of town for a summer excursion with friends, he passed through the area without thinking of that experience or noticing what had changed and how. Only on the return journey did it occur to him, and he felt rather sad about his forgetfulness. But not for long. As time went by, the memory continued to fade.

Nor did it return in 1939, when he and his parents left for the United States, where his father had been appointed director of the Boston Philharmonic, and he was to study classical philology, nor did it speak up soon after that, when Hitler invaded Poland and the war began.

All the news from Europe in that period was so monstrous and at the same time so far away that one couldn't think about it in specific terms, in detail—it was simply impossible to imagine. One thought in general—about the devastation, the victims and the appalling crimes. And also in terms of global politics and military strategy. How long would it go on for? Would the balance of power change? When would America finally enter the fray? In thoughts of this kind there was no room for details, sentiment or fond memories. Nor was there time, in any case. Life was so absorbing in these new circumstances.

But that August day suddenly came back to him in the late autumn of 1944, when the news arrived—by a long, roundabout route—of Uncle Oskar's death. He'd been killed in the Warsaw Uprising, fighting in Żoliborz. His father was on the one hand distressed by this loss, and on the other annoyed. He'd asked Oskar to join them so many times! He'd sent him some gold coins and organized transport. But Oskar had insisted on staying put. He'd said he had to stay there and fight, to defend everything he'd been building for years. How can one be so naïve, so foolhardy—quite insane! He'd always reproached him for that uncritical enthusiasm. In vain, unfortunately.

That was when, for the first time in years, he returned to that expedition, realizing how long it was since he'd last thought about it. But this did nothing to change the position of the recollection on the horizon of his memory. Quite soon it went back to its old place again—distant, not visited, wreathed in its own special mist. The current of life once again proved stronger.

After the war his father's situation gradually began to weaken. It wasn't clear why. Perhaps his advancing age was the deciding factor? Suffice it to say that he had to wave goodbye to his well-paid job and find work elsewhere. First they had to move to a different apartment, and then into the provinces. His studies were over too, for lack of money to pay for them. Faced with this crisis, they even thought of returning to Poland, but dropped the idea, chiefly because his mother had no desire to go back at all. She feared Russia like wildfire, and she was certainly right: the news from across the ocean, from behind the Iron Curtain, was terrifying. Rare letters from Warsaw from their few old friends, usually smuggled via the diplomatic post, confirmed the worst and strongly warned against deciding to return. Finally they stopped vacillating and stayed in America.

Classical philology, which he studied in Boston, was meant to be merely an introduction to archaeology (a field that was making great progress at the time), but on its own it was a ball and chain. What could one do with it? Teach Latin in schools? Ply the dismal trade of tutoring? He wasn't keen on that. He decided not to work in the profession for now, but to earn a better income, and later on, once he was on firmer ground, to take up his studies again and fulfil his aspirations.

He did that, but never went back to college. Earning a living soon became an addiction, and in time a necessity. He hired himself out wherever possible, to various offices, legal firms and other such businesses, where he wrote reports and speeches for the bosses or produced quarterly balance sheets. He became highly proficient at it, and was quite soon a valued specialist, courted with the offer of an annual bonus and a longer-than-usual vacation. Then he would go on a trip, most readily somewhere by the sea to sort out his life at last, that is to mobilize himself to change it and start over again, in keeping with his ambitions and desires. But nothing ever came of it. As soon as his vacation was over, he'd fall back into the rut of his usual work, and into the monotonous routine imposed by it. He even failed to make the change after his father died, leaving him a large share of his savings. He didn't have the energy to do it any more, and besides, it was too late. Go back to college after forty? Try to achieve something on completely new ground, where on top of that there was huge competition? Drum up enough enthusiasm? Summon up the will? He no longer had it.

His private life hadn't worked out well either. To begin with, he was very shy, which greatly limited his social interactions. And later, once he'd finally rid himself of his inhibitions, there was still something stopping him from forming lasting relationships. He was afraid of becoming dependent, he was still considering his plans, which he wouldn't be able to realize if he had a family to support, and responsibility for others filled him with anxiety. So he kept putting it off for later. 'Gently does it, I still have time,' he told himself again and again. And paid for this resistance with several break-ups, which cost him. Finally it was too late. He was left on his own, going to seed. He had let his looks go.

It was at this point, soon after he reached seventy-five, that the same childhood memory came back to him again, this time for a strange reason. In a second-hand bookshop he'd come across an album of metaphysical paintings by Giorgio de Chirico. Of course he knew this work, but he'd never taken much interest in it before. Now, for some unknown reason, it gripped his attention with special force. All those famous paintings with abstract titles: *The Enigma of a Day*, *The Enigma of an Hour*, *The Melancholy of a Street*, *The Nostalgia of the Infinite*, or *The Anguish of Departure*—he gazed as if bewitched at paintings of deserted cities, full of arcades, turrets and mysterious shadows, sunlit, lifeless and plunged in silence. He had the bizarre feeling that he knew these scenes from somewhere, as if he'd seen them before, not just on canvas or paper but in real life. Where could it have been? In Italy? On a Greek island? For a long time he failed to grasp the reference point. Until suddenly, thanks to the words 'autumn afternoon', or was it 'the enigma of autumn'?... or maybe 'the enigma of an autumn afternoon'—the words in one of these titles—he finally had a brainwave. But of course! It was that landscape of the small-scale city under construction! That uninhabited terrain with the bright hangar of the boiler house and the slender brick chimney!

He bought the little album, and then another, much larger one too, with a better selection of reproductions of de Chirico's works. He examined them closely, in an attempt to revive the memory of that day. Finally he succeeded, and scraps of foggy images began to emerge from somewhere in his mind. Individual details split off from the rest—the solid block of the boiler house, and the chimney, with the narrow iron staircase spiralling up it to the gallery. He got quite involved in these exercises in the archaeology of memory. The more he dug out of it, the more unsatisfied he felt. What had it really been like there? He wanted to check and make sure. See it once again. Return to the past for a while.

Although he shunned the Internet, he started to make use of it. Taking various routes, via a range of entries and subjects, he tried to find something that would satisfy this ludicrous need. At last he discovered the illustration he seemed to be looking for: a fairly sharp photograph of the boiler house and chimney from roughly the right period. Oh yes, that was it! Exactly the same view. He felt as if he were there again: as if he were climbing the stairs with Uncle Oskar, then at the top, pressing his hands against the cold, rounded railing, now looking down, and now into the distance.

Did the chimney still exist? And if so, what did it look like? He started scouring the Internet again, but apart from a brief note saying that there used to be a cinema in the boiler-house annex, he found nothing else.

The reawakened memory gave him no peace. What if he were to go there, it suddenly dawned on him. Not just go there in particular, but visit the city of his childhood and adolescence. He'd never been back since leaving, almost sixty years ago! Wasn't it time for an epilogue? How much time did he have left? But he couldn't make up his mind. He was afraid of the long journey and of unforeseen difficulties, and that made him dither. Instead of getting a grip and taking action, he sat in front of the computer, thinking of more and more subjects to search for online.

One day he typed Uncle Oskar's details into the Google box: first name, surname, title, Warsaw Uprising, Żoliborz. A list of about fifteen sites appeared. But he found nothing in them beyond what he already knew: engineer, urban planner, designer of housing estates and streets; killed in the Warsaw Uprising during the fighting in Żoliborz. But as well as these links, at least four or five came up that sent him to someone with the same first name and surname, but couldn't be referring to his uncle; in the first place, this namesake of his was still alive—he was born much later on, in 1945—and was a historian by profession, the author of books and articles on some local topics.

What an astonishing coincidence. Neither the first name nor the surname were common. Was it pure chance? What had prompted people with the same surname to give their child the same unusual first name as his uncle? In 1945! Soon after his death.

He trawled the Internet in search of an explanation, but in vain. Finally he wrote a letter to the editor of a local journal that had published texts by his uncle's namesake, and asked for his address, ideally his email address, 'because I'd like to send him some relevant information about one of the things he has described'. The reply came at once—from the man he was looking for. He asked how he could help. What was the thing in question?

'We have the same surname,' he explained succinctly. 'Rather a rare one in Poland. On top of that, you have the same first name as my uncle, an architect and urban planner associated with Żoliborz. Is it just chance, an unusual coincidence, or . . . ' He broke off like that, without spelling things out.

The reply confirmed his vague intuition, and greatly surpassed his boldest conjecture. Uncle Oskar's namesake was his own son—from an unofficial relationship with a nurse involved in the Uprising, who had named the child after his late father, and in time, with the help of people who'd been witnesses to their relationship, had also made sure their son carried his surname. She had acted not just in memory of her fiancé but also for practical reasons. She was counting on this hallmark that linked the child with a man who'd distinguished himself on behalf of the city to help him in life, and in the short term to help her to obtain a flat in the ruined capital. She was not mistaken: the mark of kinship worked. She'd soon been given accommodation in one of the pre-war Warsaw Housing Cooperative blocks. She had died long ago, but the flat was still in his possession. That was where he was living—her only son.

'So we're cousins,' he wrote back at once, 'and very close ones. There's no point in delaying—we should meet. Au revoir in Warsaw.'

III

He had no problem deciding where to stay. As soon as he spotted a hotel symbol on the map of the centre close to the house where he'd lived before the war, he chose it without hesitation, all the more since it wasn't expensive. It was the Hotel Gromada, side on to the square, which was now called Warsaw Insurgents Square. He asked for a room on the top floor facing the courtyard, because he needed quiet. In fact it was to have a view of the façade of his house (including his bedroom window) because, as he could tell from the photo gallery, the windows on the courtyard side of the upper floors of the hotel overlooked it. This request was accommodated.

He only told his cousin an approximate date of arrival, adding that he would be in touch as soon as he got there. He didn't want to meet up with him straight after landing. He wanted to confront the city on his own, assimilate it one to one. He wanted to be relaxed and free of stress before their first meeting.

These hopes were dashed. He had misjudged his own powers. The overnight flight and the time change proved extremely tiring, and his encounter with the city a frustrating experience. He returned from his first short stroll feeling drained and downcast. He hardly recognized a thing, and almost got lost. He found everything alien, repulsive and unspeakably ugly. He walked back to the hotel as if he were escaping to it—weary, fearful, with the painful feeling that the whole journey was pointless.

Time brought no improvement. He woke in the middle of the night, unable to sleep, and had a cup of tea; finally he took a sleeping pill that allowed him to nod off, but he only woke again at one in the afternoon, feeling tired and numb, as if his head were full of cotton wool. He didn't fancy getting up, and the thought of going outside filled him with anxiety. He had his meals and drinks brought to his room. He sat by the window in his dressing gown, staring endlessly into the third-floor window of the corner building on Hortensja Street (which was now called Górski Street)—the window of his bedroom in childhood and adolescence.

In those days, decades ago, when he'd looked out of it, he'd been facing north; now, gazing into it, he was looking the opposite way. This reversal of viewpoint seemed to him significant. In those days what he could see best was the large post office building, a link with the outside world. Now he could see the wall and his bedroom window—the vantage point of that era sending him back into the past. But entering that past was just as impossible as getting inside the flat, now the property of someone he didn't know. That sort of journey in time couldn't even be dreamed of, for what would it actually involve? What was the real point of it?

Did it mean becoming that ten-year-old again? That would have been no use at all, beyond being him again—just the same as then, unaware of the future. And so maybe it was just the outside world that should return to the same state as years ago, while he, coming up to eighty, remained who he was? No, that wasn't it either. As a visitor from the future in the world of that era, he'd be someone absent, transparent, impossible to recognize. Just as the future occupant of this hotel room was now invisible. And assuming people pass on much faster than things, that bygone world could prove lifeless, completely depopulated, and on his tour of it he'd be entirely alone, like the solitary figures in de Chirico's paintings. None of these notions was what he wanted. So what did he actually want? What would have the power to relieve his incomprehensible sense of nostalgia?

He finally summoned up the strength to call his cousin.

He'd arrived, he said, giving his voice a jolly, altogether jaunty tone, and was at the Hotel Gromada on Warsaw Insurgents Square. He'd like to invite him for lunch there. He'd be waiting by the entrance or at the reception desk.

Although at this point in time his cousin was much older than his uncle as he remembered him from before the war, he recognized him unmistakably. In a green zip-up jacket, jeans and aviator boots he had the air of a vagabond or an eternal boy scout. His manner, and in particular his way of speaking, confirmed this impression. He was direct and easy-going, jumping from one topic to the next. But everything he said was poisoned by politics, as if life had no other tones and shades. His childhood amid the ruins of Warsaw, the nightmares of Stalinism, indoctrination at school, the omnipresence of the secret police.

Time divided by the dates of the crises and follies of the communist regime. 'Rock bursts', 'crisis points', and 'turning the screw'. A constant battle, endless resistance and rebellion, the recurring phantom of Soviet interference.

Plainly the cousin was up to his ears in it all, to a point of obsession, but at the same time he was a disappointed, embittered man. Even though the country had regained independence a decade ago, and 'the Russkies have finally got out of here', he still bore a grudge, he still had it in for someone. He thought the country was going 'in the worst possible direction', that it had 'all gone wrong', that 'yet again, for the umpteenth time the opportunities have been squandered'. And as a result he felt his life had been wasted—why had he spent all those years fighting the fight, taking risks and catching it in the neck?

Don Quixote, the eternal Don Quixote, he thought as he listened to it all. The image of Uncle Oskar, except that his uncle had been positive, while his son was negative.

'Your father was an optimist,' he said at last with a smile. 'An enthusiast, even. He looked into the future with hope. He believed the world was changing for the better, not the worse.'

'So what? He miscalculated!' declared the cousin. 'Anyway, in those days, before the war, life was completely different and you could believe in something.'

He realized there was no point in polemicizing. He brought up his own concern.

'In 1929,' he began out of the blue, 'your father once took me to the Żoliborz district, which was under construction at the time. You live somewhere around there, if I've got it right...'

'Yes, all my life,' confirmed Oskar Junior with a note of rancour.

'So I have a request for you: could you take me there? I'm very curious to see how it looks now.'

'Pretty much the same, but yes, be my guest.'

'I'd especially like to see the boiler house with the brick chimney—apparently it's still there.'

'The boiler house on Suzin Street?' wondered cousin Oskar.

'I don't know what street it's on. There weren't any streets yet then.'

'That's an odd wish. Why exactly there?'

'Hard to say. Memory. It plays such tricks on us. We have no idea why we remember some things better than others. Maybe because we climbed to the top of the chimney... up some spiral stairs, to a narrow gallery, from where the view was almost like looking from an aeroplane. I'd never seen anything like it before. And there was a strange atmosphere too; the place was empty, sleepy, deserted, although there was building work going on. And that completed but as yet inactive boiler house...'

'It's inactive again now,' said the cousin with a mocking smile, 'and has been for ages. They hooked us up to the thermal power station long ago. That technological wonder has been working for thirty years at most. And they took down the staircase and the gallery straight after the war. So the folks wouldn't be able to see too much.'

When lunch was over they got up and headed for the exit. At the door the cousin announced that he was 'motorized' and the car was parked on Warecka Street. It turned out to be a battered old Fiat 500 in a pale cream colour.

'Your father was thinking of getting a car of this make,' he said, once they were on their way. 'And he promised me that as soon as he'd bought it he'd take me to that building site again so I could see the progress. But he didn't buy one in the end, and I never went there again. That promise of his is only being kept now, seventy years later. The construction work finished long ago, you're taking me, not he, and yet we're going there in a Fiat.'

'More like a parody of one. But I can't afford anything better,' said the cousin. 'At least it doesn't burn much petrol.'

They drove along the Vistula embankment, crossing the East-West Road.

'All this was destroyed,' said Cousin Oskar, pointing his left hand at the Old Town. 'The castle, the cathedral, the houses...one big ruin. I remember it being rebuilt for years on end and how the propaganda of the day boasted about it. "Reconstruction of the capital! The Old Town will be back!" Naturally the campaign was mostly for show, to pull the wool over our eyes, as if Warsaw would be the same as in the past. But in fact it was going to be different. The plan to reconstruct the centre was soon dropped. The real plan was to make a break with the past and build a new city on the ruins of the old one, a different, "socialist" one, in the style of the Palace of Culture and Science, our "gift" from Stalin. Luckily it didn't come to that, but even so they did quite enough to disfigure the city centre. Because it's not just that wedding cake right in the middle, that Russki waste-of-space with a gilded spire, it's entire developments too, the Muranów area, the Marszałkowska Housing District and many other places. And as for the houses in the Old Town, that was the height of ambition at the time. Everyone wanted to live there. Most of all those who'd implemented the city reconstruction plan in socialist style, or at any rate those who supported that idea. Well, to create a "brave new world" you've got to have comfortable conditions to work in—not in Soviet proletarian style, but in old-fashioned, bourgeois, decadent style. Wouldn't you call it decadence to live in a cosy little street in the Old Town, with all the conveniences and the atmosphere of a long bygone era, especially for a communist?'

The cousin's voice quivered with toxic irony. Altogether it sounded as if he weren't talking to him, but to some other person, with whom he'd been conducting a heated debate, piled high with layer upon layer of derision and rhetorical jibes for years.

He couldn't understand all these long-winded tirades. He wondered, listened, and said nothing. Meanwhile they drove under Starzyński Bridge.

'The Citadel,' said Cousin Oskar, returning to his commentary. 'That has survived of course. And you might think the image of that place, or rather its historical meaning will never change. Wasn't the tsarist regime an evil? Wasn't it toppled by a victorious revolution? And weren't the people who spent years fighting against that tyranny and who died at its hands heroes? And yet the whole story sounds wrong somehow. It puts too much stress on the national cause and burdens Russia with the blame, not the social system. That should be changed. But how do you do that? You can't simply deny over a hundred years of history. What you should ask is this: So what was on this site after independence, after 1918? Weren't there still some barracks, housing various troops in charge of security? Exactly, but whose? That's right, they were for the safety of the bourgeoisie, the exploitative regime. So the tyranny carried on, just like under the tsar. Because as Marxism sees it there's no difference. And to demonstrate, we come up with facts that are meant to prove it. Namely that here people were persecuted if they fought for progress and social justice. What sort of people were they? Everyone knows—they were communists. But in fact none of the famous activists was held here. Though there was one spectacular incident. In 1925 three members of the Polish Communist Party were shot here. A nasty business, for sure, like any execution, and what's more they were young people. All right, but who were they? That Hibner fellow, Rutkowski and Kniewski, that's who we're talking about. And what were they shot for? Well, this valiant trio were members of a group that carried out assassinations and terrorist acts. The one in charge, the oldest, Hibner, had been working for the Soviets from the very start of Poland's independence and had been trained for revolutionary work in Moscow itself. At the moment when he was captured he was in Poland illegally, without any Polish papers. And for what deed did they get such a severe sentence? It must have been something commendable and sublime. Acts of sabotage, perhaps? Or maybe for bumping someone off? Some "enemy of the people"? No, not even that. Oh yes, they were going to shoot another commie whom they regarded as a secret agent, but it didn't come to that. Instead they shot six random people dead: a mother and her child, a student and three policemen, and wounded another five. Incidentally, it all happened somewhere on

Zgoda, Bracka and Chmielna Streets, near your home. Didn't you hear about it?'

'I don't recall,' he said rather wearily.

'Anyway, they were sentenced to death for it,' Cousin Oskar tirelessly continued, 'and after the war the commies made martyrs of them. And on such a grand scale! They renamed streets in their honour, including Chmielna Street, where the student was killed! Lots of buildings around the country were named after them, and here, where they were killed, on the slopes of the Citadel, a monument was erected in their memory of a kind you've probably never seen. We can drive up to it, I'll show you, you'll see...'

'Maybe later, not now,' he timidly replied.

'A massive tomb, a real mausoleum. And this whole surrounding area was called Hibner Park. Just imagine— named after a Soviet agent! Over there we have Traugutt, and here Hibner, almost side by side! Incredible, a heroic insurgent and a commie terrorist equalized by death at the Citadel!'

By now they were driving along Krasiński Street, past Żeromski Park. Ahead of them, Wilson Square was gradually coming into view.

'Would you like to get out here somewhere or drive straight to the spot?' asked the cousin, stopping at the lights before a junction.

'There was a little street here, where the tram stopped. It was called Ustronie...Behind a large house with a front like a ship.'

'Ah, you mean Toeplitz Street,' said the cousin nodding. 'It's called Toeplitz now. But the tram doesn't stop there any more, or even run that way.'

'Never mind, let's drive up there. I'd like to look around. And then we can continue on foot.'

'Very good,' said the cousin, and drove into Wilson Square.

He took a good look around, to left and right, but recognized nothing. It was all so different: the trams, the buses, the traffic, the people. Another world, another place.

'In communist Poland this square had its name changed too,' said Cousin Oskar in a scathing tone as he stopped at the lights again. 'They renamed it Paris Commune Square. They only restored Wilson a short time ago. In your honour,' he added, 'a visitor from America.'

Though not amused, he smiled weakly. They turned into Krasiński Street and then into Toeplitz.

'It's here,' said the cousin, parking his small Fiat facing the gate into a yard behind the ship-house.

They got out of the car and crossed the street.

He looked around in search of the chimney, but couldn't find it. To the left rose a church, to the right a tower block with a red sign saying 'Merkury', and straight ahead a fence stretched along the pavement, with some bushes and small trees behind it.

'There's a nice little school on the left,' said the cousin ironically, 'and a nice little market on the right. And here we live our nice little lives . . . '

'So where is the boiler house?' he couldn't resist asking. 'Or at least which way is it? I remember having it in clear view from this spot. When your father brought me here he covered my eyes so I wouldn't catch sight of it too soon.'

'No fear, it's there,' the cousin reassured him. 'You'll see it in a moment. That house is hiding it from view.' He pointed at a white building on the far side of a small square.

They strolled towards Krasiński Street.

'And here you have the church where in Solidarity's time Father Popiełuszko held his famous masses for the homeland, for which they battered him to death, and where he's now buried. Even the pope came here on one of his pilgrimages. You may have heard about it . . . '

'Of course,' he agreed for the sake of peace.

'Why is it,' continued Cousin Oskar, 'that we're only known in the outside world for that sort of incident? Though so many things that happened here were to do with hope, there was so much optimism! But all that got through to the world was this . . . mainly this, because there was also Gdańsk Station, thanks to the Jewish exodus in the late 1960s. At the time it was mockingly dubbed the Umschlagplatz...'

'You're exaggerating, you're blowing it up,' he interrupted irritably, but his cousin didn't stop.

'My mother told me about the time they brought Picasso here, in 1948 when he was in Poland for the Peace Congress. To show him the so-called Glass House on Mickiewicz Street, which was actually built before the war, in 1938, I think. As if to say we had fabulous architecture in the style of Le Corbusier too: ultra-modernist, avant-garde, "Western". They gave an exclusive party for him there on the roof. Small tables, snacks, coffee, French wine. So the maestro would appreciate it and never forget! He'd go away dazzled and make us famous worldwide! So Picasso had a bit of a look, nodded, did some prattling, smoked a cigarette, and left a dog end. Which was kept for years like a holy relic... God, how pitiful it all is, how embarrassing! Then there was the time when Munk filmed *Bad Luck* at several locations around here,' Cousin Oskar went on with rising fervour. 'That I remember, because I bunked off from school to watch the filming for hours on end. And I heard what people were saying to each other then. "Never mind what it's about. What matters is that part of our house will be visible!" And once the film was in the cinemas, they mainly went to see those shots. They went again and again, hoping it'd be famous, go to Cannes, to the festival, and have a global career. And then "part of their house" would be seen everywhere, out there, in the great world outside, people would know that somewhere over there Dobchinsky and Bobchinsky are living... Unfortunately the film didn't achieve global fame—it was too subtle, too refined for that. And probably because it wasn't full of shocking defeat and sacrifice, like Wajda's *Kanał*, for instance, or his *Ashes and Diamonds*. Those films won prizes.'

'Why are we going this way, along this wide avenue?' he asked, quite unconcerned about failing to react to his cousin's stories at all. 'You said it was somewhere over there,' he said, pointing at a white building on Filarecka Street.

'Because that's where it is,' replied Cousin Oskar. 'And in the past, years ago, you could take a shortcut, through the housing estate backyard. But now it's all fenced off or blocked by passages, under the pretext of order and supposedly for security. So either you have to have a key, or an intercom code, otherwise you can't get through. I don't have either, and that's why we have to go round.'

They walked a while in silence. He, slightly stooping, in a light, unbuttoned overcoat, and his taller cousin, in his shabby green jacket. Although there was a gap of twenty-five years between them they didn't look very different in age. They were both 'old' by now; each was well past his prime.

It was fine weather, October sunshine, the end of a golden autumn.

'This whole area,' said Cousin Oskar, with a vague semi-circular gesture, 'changed very little for a long time after the war. Not much was built, just a few houses, and that according to designs from before the occupation. All the energy went into rebuilding the city centre. And as a result, in this place, on this semi-feral terrain, time came to a halt. Naturally, as a child I never noticed. For me that was the normal state of affairs, business as usual. But for older people, of your generation, compared with the destruction of almost the entire centre this area was like an oasis, an outdoor museum, a lost world. And they sometimes came here to feel "like before the war". I was always hearing those words. But the "progressives", who went along with the new regime, were put off by it. They didn't like this "rural dump", this "squalid district", because although it was built according to modern designs, like the exemplary Gdynia, it still preserved the climate of the "mistaken past". Especially at the military and civil service estates, in those mini mansions, villas and rows of elegant houses. That's exactly why that area was condemned to stagnation. At the time it was as if things would be like that here forever. And it was hopeless. But when something did begin to change, when traces of the past started to disappear from the streets and houses, because some of them had been renovated, and especially built onto, people regretted that suddenly something was missing, the connection with that mythical time "before the war" was gone. Now there's none of it left at all.'

They turned right into Suzin Street.

'All right, now look out,' said Cousin Oskar, resuming his derisive tone, 'we're approaching our destination. Should I shield your eyes?'

'No, thank you, I can manage,' he replied with a smile, concealing his rising emotion.

As they advanced, the back wall of the boiler house gradually came into view on their right. Finally the tip of the chimney appeared above its roof. Slender, with no gallery, but instead it was spiked with numerous antennas for wireless networks.

He stopped and craned his neck. Cousin Oskar stopped too, and looked up at the chimney, as if wanting to find out what it was about it that he hadn't noticed before that could stir so much fascination. But he couldn't see anything to fit the bill. Finally he let his head drop, shrugged, and stood still in silence, as if to respect his kinsman's contemplation. But it didn't last long. Faced with the wall, which had an arched top and was scored by narrow vertical windows, he couldn't refrain from saying: 'Well, then? What do you think? Can you see any change?'

'Of course I can,' he replied without hesitation. 'Anyway, you forewarned me—the gallery is missing. And instead of a staircase the chimney is girded with hoops. As if it were going to fly apart. That wasn't there either.'

'I don't mean the chimney, I mean this wall. Can't you see the difference?'

'My good fellow, think about it! I've only seen it once before, and that was almost seventy years ago!'

'You should spot it without ever having seen this wall before. It's so glaring. Just look: how many windows are there, those narrow slits? Five. And they're bisected by gaps at the top. And how many were there originally? There were three! Three lovely vertical features, flawlessly designed! They've even spoiled that.'

He squinted, trying to imagine it. And suddenly, in some strange dimension, not exactly outside or inside himself, he really did get a glimpse of the old boiler-house back wall with its three narrow stripes glazed from within, and how dazzlingly white it looked in the sharp, August sunlight, like a huge shield with a coat of arms engraved on it. It was a bizarre image: miraculous and mysterious, prompting delight and dread. A factory in the wilderness. A hangar with a chimney in the middle of a field. Why? For whom? For what purpose? In an abandoned world. Defunct? Or not yet born?

He woke from his reverie, walked slowly ahead and crossed Próchnik Street. Only now did he notice that what from a distance had looked like a dark, fuzzy stain, was actually a stone slab fixed to the wall—a commemorative plaque. He ran his eyes down the inscription. 'In memory of the soldiers of Dąbrowski Battalion within the military units of the PPS who lost their lives fighting the Nazi invader ... for independence ... socialism ... in the first battle of the Uprising ...'

'This is where the Uprising began?' he wondered at the sight of that word.

'By pure accident,' explained the cousin. 'It was meant to start somewhere else, and several hours later. The shooting here wasn't planned. But it's of no significance. What matters is what's in the inscription. Did you read it carefully?'

He ran his gaze down the metal letters again, but he couldn't see anything remarkable about it. He spread his hands helplessly and cast an inquiring glance.

'Who organized the Uprising?' said Cousin Oskar, like a teacher clarifying the whole matter. 'We know it was the Armia Krajowa—the Home Army, which in the communist era no one was allowed to talk about, except to criticize it. Like the Uprising itself. No monuments were erected to those who took part in it. Only after the political thaw of October 1956 did things begin to ease up. So as soon as they sensed that, the handful of survivors launched an effort to erect a plaque that would feature at least those two letters, the symbolic "AK" to stand for the Home Army: it's here, right at the bottom. Negotiating with the authorities took several months. Finally it was agreed, but on one condition: that the inscription would say that those who were killed here were mainly connected with the Socialist Party, and that they were fighting not just for freedom and independence but also for socialism. That's why the letters PPS, for the Polish Socialist Party, and the word "socialism" appear, so that right at the end the letters AK could also be there. Charming, you must admit...I remember when they put it up.'

'Did your father die here?' he asked in dismay, realizing that if that were the case, it would be a truly ironical twist of fate.

'If he'd lost his life here,' replied Cousin Oskar, 'I wouldn't be here now. Because I wouldn't exist. Or I'd have been someone else, which comes to the same thing. This is where the Uprising began. He was killed right at the end of it.'

'And you were born...'

'I don't like thinking about it or going back to the past, so let's drop it.'

'Of course, I'm sorry,' he said, nervously raising his hands in a gesture of capitulation. 'Can one still go right up to the chimney?' he said, changing the subject. 'Surely there's a way in?'

'Of course there is,' came the reply, 'but is it open? As I've told you, around here they like to fence everything off and block access. We'll find out in a moment.' He continued down Suzin Street, along the side wall of the boiler house.

It was crenellated, like the battlements of a castle. The concrete beams supporting its arched vault were a bit like ribs, as if all that were left of some original structure was the skeleton. He felt strange walking past this building. At one point he ran a finger over the stone wall, discreetly, so the cousin wouldn't see. 'It's me. I'm here again,' he thought childishly. 'Do you recognize me? Do you remember?'

'Look what they did here!' said Oskar, who was slightly ahead, and beckoned to him. 'Look how they've spoiled this!'

Beyond the long wall of the boiler house stood a narrower building with a sign saying RAINBOW CINEMA. Indeed, without knowing what this quaint annex had originally looked like it was plain to see that it had been altered. Everything about it was heavy, clumsy and shoddy, contrasting with the architecture of the boiler house which, though industrial—austere and sombre—did have character and perfect proportions.

'To be sure,' he said, 'it's not stunningly beautiful.'

'Not stunningly beautiful!' said Oskar, laughing. 'That's a funny way of putting it. It's simply monstrous! Especially for someone who knows what it used to look like. Apart from the Polonia this was the only functioning cinema in Warsaw after the war! Half the city used to come here. There were queues for tickets and the touts did a roaring trade. There was actually something going on! Especially on summer evenings. There was no ventilation in the projectionist's booth, so he'd open a small window. And then you could hear not just the reel whirring but also snippets of the soundtrack—dialogues in Russian, Polish, French and even English. And that brought all sorts of poor hopefuls here, who hadn't the money for a ticket, or had already seen the film but wanted to relive the experience. So they'd stand out here for hours, tensely listening to the muffled voices and sounds, trying to imagine what was showing on the screen. And to picture the world outside, that whole other world. Just for a while…just in their dreams…to be somewhere else, not here—.' Cousin Oskar broke off abruptly, as if ashamed of something, and gazed oddly to one side. But he soon returned to his previous stance and added calmly: 'And what was stopping them?'

'It's the passage of time that's upset you, not the alteration of this building,' he said. 'Do you think that if the cinema had stayed the same you wouldn't be feeling as you feel now, years on? You'd feel the same thing, maybe even more strongly. Because that sort of ossified world may let one enter its space, but it doesn't let one enter its time. And that's rather distressing.'

'I prefer that sort of distress to the distress of looking at this,' retorted Oskar, then walked to the end of the Rainbow Cinema building, peeked around the corner and cried: 'You're lucky, it's open!'

Through a half-open gate for delivery vehicles they entered a strange piece of ground surrounded by fence panels, not exactly a driveway and not exactly a yard for storing junk. It was a mess—there were planks, pipes, heaps of stones and bricks lying about, as well as some old radiators, clapped-out tools and hundreds of other odds and ends. But one's gaze was immediately drawn away from all that by the massive brick chimney springing from the ground. Only here could one see how big it was. Its base was surrounded by a concrete support, roughly a metre high. That wasn't there in the past: he could remember stepping straight onto the staircase from the ground. Staring up at the top from this distance as a cloud went scudding past in the blue sky made one feel a bit dizzy, and it looked as if the chimney were toppling over.

A man in stained work clothes leaned out of a door marked 'Storehouse' and cast them a hostile glance.

'Can I help you, guys?' he said dryly.

'There's no need, man,' said Cousin Oskar sarcastically.

'What do you want?' asked the man even more fiercely. 'There's no entry here.'

'Where does it say that?' asked Oskar, clearly refusing to give way. 'The gate was open.'

'If I say there's no entry, it means there's no entry,' said the man crossly.

'You can say that,' replied Oskar, 'I'm not stopping you.'

'Listen here,' said the storehouse man, moving towards him abruptly, 'you don't talk to me like that. Please leave, or else...'

'Or else what?' said Oskar through clenched teeth, as if to pick a fight.

'Or I'll call the police or the municipal guard!'

'Go ahead, call away,' said Oskar, making light of the threat, and took out a cigarette which he calmly lit. The man in work clothes moved swiftly to the gate and started to close it. 'Here's hoping you won't regret that later, man!' Oskar shouted after him.

This piece of cheek had an extraordinary effect on the man. He seemed to carry on with his disciplinary action, pushing the gate to, but at that he stopped: he didn't padlock it, as he had clearly been intending to, but left it unlocked, if not slightly ajar. Then he strode rapidly back into the storehouse, making it plain to the intruders that he was going to summon help, on the spot or by phone.

'Why didn't you tell him we're on a trip down memory lane and we'd just like to take a look at the chimney?' he said to his cousin.

'Why would I? What does he care?'

'There wouldn't have been a row.'

'He has no right to question us or to chase us out of here. I'm not going to explain myself to a bastard like that.'

'But what if he really does call the police?'

'Don't worry, he won't. He's already pretty scared he's trodden on a mine. And if he has run off to complain to the manager, he's really going to be in for it!' Oskar took a mobile phone from his pocket and went off aside with it.

He was left alone beneath the chimney. He didn't know what to do. The whole mood associated with coming to this place had evaporated in an instant. He couldn't focus on anything. He looked at the things scattered all around, glanced at Oskar, who with a sour smirk was talking to someone on the phone, and wandered to and fro. Until suddenly, on the chimney wall, about three metres off the ground, he spotted a blackish streak, climbing up a short stretch of it like a snake. He took a closer look at it. Oh yes, that was it, without a doubt: a rusty mark left by part of the staircase up to the gallery. From this point he started to move his gaze up the chimney, and in one or two places he thought he could see similar traces of the spiral staircase on the red brickwork. Once he reached the top, he felt his head spin. He sat down cautiously on the edge of the concrete support, took a deep breath and closed his eyes.

'But slowly, very slowly,' he heard the gentle voice of the moustachioed man in overalls rising from the depths, 'because it makes you dizzy'. Yes, it did, he thought to his amusement, without going up it.

And it occurred to him that that good-natured, jovial watchman with the moustache who had let him into the staircase seventy years ago, with a friendly warning about the twisting steps, had actually been warning him about life. Because that day, up at the top, although the gallery seemed to sway in the wind, he hadn't felt dizzy; before him lay fields, lots of empty space that was just starting to be filled systematically. But now, as he sat at the bottom, on the concrete support, his head was spinning, and the sight before him was of a rubbish tip. And the watchman's successor, a stern man in work clothes, was now summoning the security to remove him from here.

Why is my head in such a muddle? he thought in confusion. I haven't lived fast, have I? On the contrary, I've lived very slowly, perhaps too slowly. I kept putting off climbing all sorts of ladders for later, until it was too late. Maybe that's the reason why? Maybe one should speed up and live life to the limits, until one's head goes spinning, because only then does a sense of calm come at the end? Whatever the case, it has been and gone, it's behind me now.

Yes, it had all happened. The new district had come into being. Żoliborz—*joli bord*, pretty riverbank. And he had returned to this spot, to find out the 'effect of the works'. To know about the 'works and days'. And suddenly he caught a glimpse of himself, sitting beneath that chimney with no staircase or gallery in the late autumn sun, and the whole world around him—all those streets and squares, and the modest houses in modernist style— was empty and deserted. As if uninhabited. Just like in Giorgio de Chirico's *The Anguish of Departure*.

The Warsaw Map (2001)

Zbigniew Mentzel

For years and years, on an annual basis I bought myself the new updated issue of the 'Warsaw Map' produced by the State Cartographic Publishing Enterprise; studying the street index and the urban transport routes was one of the many activities in which I took genuine pleasure.

Although I have lived in Warsaw since the day I was born, I have never seen the panorama of my native city, but just once, in early childhood, I came close to it. I can remember the winter's day when my father took me to the Palace of Culture and promised we'd ride up in the lift to the thirtieth floor to see the view of Warsaw in all directions of the compass. We stood in the queue for tickets to the viewing terrace. But it turned out he hadn't any money.

Just before the ticket desk my father started feverishly fumbling in his pockets. While we were on the tram, the Warsaw thieves had extracted his coin purse from his coat, a black souvenir purse shaped like a horseshoe that he always carried for luck. We walked away from the ticket desk with our tails between our legs. On Parade Square my father fretted over the loss of his talisman. I didn't know how to console him.

Not having seen Warsaw from on high, I gradually inspected it from below, at first by taking a close look underfoot at the Warsaw pavements, roadways, tramlines and manhole covers, and then in time lifting my gaze more boldly to take in the Warsaw streetlamps, shops and churches, and the sombre architecture of the central government buildings.

During our Sunday walks my father would show me Warsaw's monuments, with special consideration for the ones that allowed him to demonstrate his anti-Soviet feelings. Sometimes I thought he overdid it. For instance, when with a sarcastic smirk he assured me that the athletes in sports singlets on the bas-relief outside the Tenth Anniversary Stadium represented ragged refugees from the East, I thought his interpretation was stretching it a bit.

My mother, with whom I went for walks on weekdays, was more interested in the people to be seen in Warsaw. On Warsaw's streets and in Warsaw's parks she obsessively distinguished the Varsovians (including the Varsovians going three generations back) from the non-Varsovians. In the 1950s we occupied a four-room flat, and because of the policy about surplus space, any non-Varsovian might come to live with us as a sub-tenant, forcibly quartered on us, and with a resident's registration order to boot. At some point we already had four sub-tenants, all non-Varsovians, of course, and they made my mother's life into hell. In those days the housing law prompted chauvinism among even the most open-minded Varsovians.

Once I had learned to read, I liked to take part in Warsaw's daily life by reading the newspapers *Warsaw Life* and *The Evening Express*. Both of them devoted a lot of space to such typically Varsovian rituals as washing the tunnel on the East-West Route (the major thoroughfare that crosses the city), or extracting drunks from the ditch that ran around the bear enclosure, not far from the Orthodox church and the Transfiguration of Jesus hospital.

The Warsaw Map that I bought myself each year in a new, updated edition, issued by the State Cartographic Publishing Enterprise, was of vital necessity for me to be able to chart the areas of my own interests within the boundaries of the city. In the 1960s the pastime that occupied me non-stop was amateur rod fishing, so I used the Warsaw Map to mark out the fishing spots on the Warsaw stretch of the river Vistula and the shops that sold bait and fishing gear. At least a dozen times a month, having checked the addresses in the street index, and having researched the most convenient connections on the public transport diagram, I would set off to hunt for items that were non-existent on the standard sales displays, such as Norwegian hooks made by a firm named Mustad, iridescent fishing line one tenth of a millimetre in diameter, or slender floats made of porcupine quills.

The Angler's House on State National Council Street gradually became my second home. Looking in its enormous window from the street you saw two blackboards, one showing the monthly repertoire of the Dolphin cinema, which was located in the same building, and the other showing Poland's angling records in the categories of the forty most common freshwater fish. I once shone with my own triumphant presence on this blackboard as the record holder for catching barbel! Unfortunately, a couple of months later my record was wiped out by the communist writer Jerzy Putrament.

Once I had dropped angling, from the mid-1970s I marked new and second-hand bookshops on the Warsaw map. I was particularly interested in the bookshops that sold tickets for the State Book Lottery. I played this lottery in order to lose. For every three losing tickets you were given a consolation prize, which you could choose from among some excellent books. While in the bookshops in the city's central districts the shelves stocked with consolation prizes were soon culled, expeditions to the outer suburbs proved fruitful, so I would come home from Targówek, Bielany, Wola or Bródno laden with literature that distanced me from the reality of Warsaw.

I was finally persuaded that the history of Warsaw is my own family history on reading my great-grandmother's diary. In the nineteenth century her cousin Adam, whom she loved with a sinful passion, took part in a plot to assassinate the imperial viceroy, von Berg. The plot failed, and most of the conspirators were caught on the spot and executed, while Adam disappeared without trace. One night my great-grandmother dreamed that on the orders of the imperial viceroy her cousin had been walled up alive in the central pillar of the Kierbedź Bridge that crossed the Vistula. She believed it to the end of her days. Kierbedź Bridge was blown up twice, but all the pillars survived, and when I came into the world the Śląsko-Dąbrowski Bridge was being built on them.

My great-grandmother's dream connected me with Warsaw more firmly than the bookshops marked on the city map, where nowadays I buy novels written by my contemporaries.

Che Guevara
(2001)

Olga Tokarczuk

At the time, everything happened in the dark. Can that be true? The daylight only appeared for a while, and even then it was coarse, like linen underwear, like starched student-hall bedsheets, like a sweater knitted in the autumn using synthetic rug yarn. The sun was like a huge sixty-watt lightbulb. At school leaving time it was already dark, and after that it only continued to get darker. The dimly lit, empty shops cast yellow stains on the wet pavements. Gloom in the trams, gloom from behind the curtained windows of flats on Nowotko Street. Early December. Warsaw.

The whole time I was cold. At the bus stop I dreamed of a down jacket, but it didn't exist in this dimension. Things like that were from outer space, from somewhere abroad, from a world I couldn't begin to imagine. At the university refectory, which everyone called 'The Cockroach', I would order half a plate of vegetables and a pancake. Then I'd feel high on overeating. Can I run to the expense of a doughnut? Once I'm working, I dreamed, once I'm a mature woman, with a position in life, I'll buy myself a whole tray of doughnuts—on Marchlewski Avenue—because that's where they make the best ones. I'll eat them calmly and systematically, starting with the one at the top of the pyramid.

At one of the meetings in the assembly hall the volunteers had been given special passes to leave the occupation strike, so I was privileged—I could go outside. I would proudly pick up my things from the table for sleeping and go downstairs, where the person on duty checked my name against a list, and then unlocked the door for me. There I would stand in the frosty air, in the sudden silence, in the indeterminate light that hid the secrets of the faculty garden. The buzz of conversation was gone, so was the sound of the ping-pong ball rhythmically striking the laminated table tops, and the dull clang of a guitar from the other side of a wall. Gone was the cloud of arid, dust-coated air that we all had in our throats. I inhaled the cold. My patients were my saviours; they freed me. From afar, from the Praga district they gave me absolution, which like an angel message flew across the Vistula and over the city to land on Stawki Street above my head. The soft light of the Holy Spirit. I was chosen.

As I walked to the number 111 bus stop, I'd already be stiff with cold before reaching the Umschlagplatz Monument, but once the bus arrived, I made myself quite at home in it—I would rest my feet on the bar under the seat, wrap my coat tails tightly around my thighs and hips, turn up my collar and, comforted by the warmth of my own breath, I would glide across the city, like an eye, like a pure, dark pupil.

As soon as the bus left Teatralny Square and entered Krakowskie Przedmieście, the strike at the University announced itself on red-lettered banners slung across the Philosophy Faculty building and on the university gate. Commotion, excitement, a strange euphoria, the dark silhouettes of people in clusters, stalls selling samizdat, and two boys always posted outside the philosophy building with a box into which passers-by threw cigarettes, rarely whole packs, usually single units. Over there on Stawki Street we were cut off from all that enthusiasm, hubbub, light and warmth. Our leaves were going brown as we mouldered away in that dismal building. We were the provincial strike. Bob Marley did not help by being played around the clock like a sort of revolutionary barrel-organ, like a prayer mill. The real story was happening here, on Krakowskie Przedmieście.

Through the bus window I could see the afternoon traffic on Nowy Świat Street—there was always something to be seen to, always something to see; at historical moments the herd instinct intensifies. I would get out on Nowy Świat, or travel on across the dark, indifferent Vistula to the Saska Kępa district. There the city was quiet, and the snow crunched more boldly, like in the country-side. Walking down the street was like entering the embrace of a protective woman.

I had three adults in my care. My boss, M., referred to them as 'clients'. I too said 'clients'. It would have been a betrayal to say 'patients'—that would have meant he was on the other side of the fence, on the side of conformism, of the hypocrites, on the side of the system. M. also said 'madmen', or 'lunatics', which I liked best, because it sounded rustic and familiar, as if this word took us back to the roots, to linen, cotton, and plain black bread; there was no hint of deception in them, no vapid philosophizing, no 'manic-depressive psychosis', no 'paranoid schizophrenia', or 'borderline'. Simple words could be trusted. That is the truth—people go mad, it's been happening for ever, said M. Why is that so? That's what your studies are for, here at the lectures you determine whether it's to do with genes, upbringing, subtle changes of molecules, enzymes, devils, or age-old ritual. People go mad, there's no arguing about it. It has always been the case. There have always been madmen and normal people, with us, the patient helpers, somewhere in between.

M. commanded us from the second floor of an apartment house on Tamka Street, but I rarely saw him. I was in touch with the older volunteers, who were responsible for us. It was hierarchical, because I belonged to a network. Every afternoon we were dispersed about the city like members of a secret sect, like an esoteric emergency service, like the commercial travellers of mental health. When I occasionally lost my head, I would try to imagine what M. would do in my place. He was big and bearded, always in a checked flannel shirt, leaning against the windowsill, from which he could see the entire city. The thought of him reassured me. His message was clear, though never said directly, even when we were drinking at his flat after a meeting—people suffer, because that's how the world is. But sometimes they suffer pointlessly, they make victims of themselves, though no one demands it of them and no one understands it. Our task is simply to be with them. We believe it helps them. We don't know exactly how.

I had my two points on the map—a few tree-shaded streets in Saska Kępa, and the Amatorska café on Nowy Świat Street, right by the Avenue. Here at a little table in the corner, in this café that was smoky and dark even in the fleeting light of noon in winter, I would smoke cigarettes and drink tea as I waited for Che Guevara. I usually sat at a table next to the window, through which I could see a section of the street including part of a clothes shop that was always half empty. I'd see women in shapeless checked coats with string bags like nets, hunting for a delivery of goods. My patient would come in, stamping noisily, shooting glances, fully prepared for the stage, festooned in mess tins and wound about with imitation ammunition belts, in his floor-length greatcoat and the helmet under which he wore a warm woollen cap. 'Heil Hitler!' he'd shout from the doorway. Or 'Hello, fellow workers!', or something equally absurd, and people would slowly turn to look at him and smile, not with derision nor tolerance, but more or less cordially. Sometimes someone would shout back: 'Hi, Che Guevara!' And then go back to their previous chatter.

Before reaching me he would accost a few other people, recite them a poem and then joke with the waitress as she made him a weak cup of tea with no lemon, but sickly sweet.

'She's waiting for me,' he'd announce to all, pointing a finger at me.

When at last he sat down and took off his helmet, a white, buzz-cut hairstyle appeared, and I felt as if here he was in his own theatre dressing-room. He had come off stage, put out the light and was sighing with relief.

'It's cold,' he'd say in a calm tone, warming his hands on the tea.

He'd smile. His smooth, pale, childish face didn't know how to scowl.

'So how are you?' I'd ask, and he'd reply: 'All right,' or 'Not all right', but it was probably of no significance, because what did 'all right'/'not all right' mean? In his life all judgements went their own sweet way, according to a unique design. Equally, there was no point in urging him to take the prescribed drugs, because he refused to do it.

'I'm not myself when I swallow pills,' he'd say.

M. would say that madness can be a special, weird way of adapting to the world. There's nothing wrong with it. Anything to avoid suffering pointlessly—he would add his favourite phrase, and then we would wonder: when does suffering have a point? As long as we don't let fear pacify us—pacify—that was another of his favourite words.

So my job was to take Che Guevara to hospital at the right moment, when the suffering abruptly left its safe floodplain, when it became dangerous to life, totally unbearable. When the world suddenly began to bare its fangs, turned into a monster and revealed its true face—it was always against people. My job was to lock up his flat, keep hold of the keys, then visit him on the ward, and once he was discharged to settle him back into life. And then become just one of his many spectators again, keep an eye on him as he accosted people in the street, as his strange attire stopped whole families, old ladies in hats and cotton gloves, or men on business in the capital, who fled at the sight of him, warding him off with their briefcases. Sometimes I would say goodbye to him, but continue to follow him down Nowy Świat and Rutkowski Streets; the mess tins attached to his belt would jangle, scaring away the confused pigeons. Some people treated him like a beggar and pressed a few groszy into his hand. He would take it, without looking ashamed. Once I saw him join in with a demonstration. He clowned around. He marched. He shouted 'Hände hoch!' or 'The Gestapo!', thus repeating some of the wartime recordings that filled his head—his memory didn't go into the future beyond 1945. He ignored the present day, and maybe that allowed him to feel safe— he was out of date. Nevertheless, I was afraid something bad would happen to him. Revolutions don't like lunatics, because revolutions are deadly serious.

'We can go to the club,' I would suggest, referring to the launderette converted into a dayroom where we could take our 'clients' for tea, a game of draughts or ping-pong.

'I don't like going there.'

'Why not?'

'Because they take me for a madman there.'

'You do everything to be taken for a madman.'

'I know.'

'You dress up as a partisan, you shout in the street, you accost people, you spout nonsense…'

'I know.'
'Then tell me why. Why do you do it?'
'I don't know. Maybe I am a madman.'
'Maybe you are.'

* * *

One evening, at the strike, both telephones were inundated and a huge queue formed for them. As if enchanted, Mum kept repeating the same old thing: 'Come home. Get on the train and come home.' My father would tear the receiver from her and say: 'Bring me some materials.' I'd crawl into my sleeping bag on the table by the radiator and lie there, reading. There was a couple from the year above living on the neighbouring table, but I didn't know how to talk to them. They were totally absorbed in each other.

The endless meetings in the assembly hall, the demands put to the vote, the committee chairman rapping his clogs against the concrete floor, a remainder from when the Gestapo was housed in the psychology building. And then, by the minute, that elevated atmosphere of revolution would infect me. The delicious feeling of being just a cog in the machine, a grain of sand, a tiny fraction, a snowflake that knows it's part of a blizzard. It's a relief—to be a collective being, not to belong to oneself, to lose the borders, if only for a while. We smoked cigarettes by the overflowing ashtrays in the corridor leading to the assembly hall. The clusters of smokers rippled and changed as occasionally someone came and went. And then suddenly I'd be over-whelmed by tiredness, and my need for solitude would be so great that I would lock myself in the toilet on the second floor and sit there, staring at the flakes of peeling oil paint. I'd hold my breath whenever there was a sudden yank at the door handle and then someone took their place in the next cubicle. I'd shamefully return to my table, reading Cortazar's *Hopscotch* once again, this time according to a different key, in another direction. The discovery that a sequence of events doesn't have to be fixed, and that maybe it's the same in life—events shuffle before my eyes and arrange themselves in random configurations—was thrill-ing. I would go downstairs, join the queue for the phone only to abandon it immediately and go to the buffet, from there back to the queue, and then repeat this pattern again. And then onto the table, off to the toilet, to the assembly hall, to the phone, onto the table, back to the buffet … Then I began to think others were doing it too, experimenting with order and chaos, and that explained the restless movement within the building, the little groups of people on the streets, the fluttering flags hoisted in every possible place, and the sudden, impenetrable darkness in the mid-dle of the day.

Beyond the window the city was going dark, gleaming. From over the radiator, from the table topped with a sleep-ing bag, it looked like a place where there were no friendly, human spaces any more, as if this time were tearing off the soft upholstery of the world and exposing its sharp, ugly skeletons. In an experiment, some baby monkeys were given the choice of two mock-up mothers: some were nice and soft, but had no milk; the others were cold and made of wire, but milk flowed freely from their artificial nipples. And the baby monkeys chose the exquisite softness of starving to death. Small and weak, they cuddled up to the fake fur. Last thing at night I prayed for all the creatures used in experiments. For the people too.

At the time I needed softness. My hands instinctively wandered to the plush curtains in cinemas and restaurants, they hankered after impossible chenille and velvets, stroked my corduroy trousers bald, and crumpled a faded silk scarf. I craved the softness of mild, damp spring air, sunshine, sand, real coffee and scented soap. My bones ached from sleeping on the table, and the rough neck of my sweater left a red ring on my skin.

I was also responsible for Igor. He was about my age, and he lived with his mother and father in a flat full of knick-knacks on Szasery Street. Modest and quiet, always in a good mood, he would run away from home, hopping from one train to another without a ticket. He managed to get by on these journeys—people would offer him sandwiches, apples or boiled sweets. He knew how to make a good impression. He would vanish for months at a time.

He'd come home tired and dirty. Then in a sort of fury his mother would take him to hospital, but they soon let him go. The postman would bring his allowance, and Igor would set off again on a new railway journey. Drunk on travel, on forging ahead to wherever, he showed no sign of life, until after a while he'd be brought back by the militia or an ambulance, from Ełk or Suwałki. We kept trying to plant him in one spot like a bush, we tried to hold him back. I would go to the club with him, where there were endless dreary games of cards or ludo, or people solved crosswords to a point of tedium. We offered him every potential passion—stamp-collecting, making model aeroplanes, keeping angelfish, collecting minerals. He would gently smile and return to the topic of trains. He'd ask if we could go for a walk to the station—across the bridge, then along Jerozolimskie Avenue. And so we would wander along the platforms watching the destination stations changing on the electronic boards. He would stand just behind the red line to get a close look at the trains pulling in. He would count the coaches. He knew that this train would have just one sleeper car, and that one nothing but couchettes.

'Oh, there's the restaurant car,' he'd say reverently.

'You can't go trailing about the country,' I kept telling him as if he were a child, and I some sort of universal mother.

'I know,' he'd reply like an adult.

'It's dangerous, you can't live like that. Afterwards you'll end up in hospital again.'

'Can't it be arranged for me to become a railway worker?'

'Possibly, but you'd have to go to school.'

'Can't it be done without school?' he'd ask in disappointment.

He called me 'the Queen of Poland'.

A few years later he visited my parents. He must have remembered the name of the town from our conversations. He arrived first thing in the morning, neatly dressed and polite. He said he was a friend of mine. My mum fed him breakfast, and the three of them chatted away. But as soon as Igor felt safe, he unfurled his vision of the cosmos of train connections, locomotives, stations and railway workers, a universe in motion, in eternal haste, in transit, amid clouds of gushing steam, the rasp of the points, whistles and hoots, a monotonous rumble, the press of the crowds wandering through glazed naves onto platform entrances, towards the altars of ticket windows, where the priestly brotherhood of stationmasters performed their rituals, and the conductors appeared in uniform for their retreats. Sacred end-of-the-line stations, mystical destinations, salvation through travel, through travel, through travel.

'And your daughter, the Queen of Poland, the Empress of Psychology, the Drewnica Hospital Goddess, may she be praised, may she succeed in life and after life, in death and after death, I beseech all and sundry.'

A May sun shone over the town, and the branches of a larch peeped through the kitchen window. Outside, the neighbour was sweeping the front pavement. A morsel of food suddenly stuck in my mum's throat. The cigarette came to a stop in my father's lips.

At the strike there was Cyryl. A strange, tall boy with a pimply face covered in uneven clumps of stubble. He was extremely talented, and despite being autistic, had been admitted to college by way of exception. He would glide gloomily down the corridors, causing those whom he passed to fall silent; suddenly confused, embarrassed by their own prattle, they would turn their eyes to the painted walls, stub out their cigarettes or suddenly start reading a noticeboard. During the stormy meetings in the assembly hall Cyryl would stand in a corner, staring at a point on the floor a few metres ahead of the tips of his shoes. We would involuntarily follow his gaze, looking for a mark, a piece of paper or a small coin on the floor. But he was staring at nothing. He was cared for from a distance by B., whom the students adored. She constantly reminded us of the need for tolerance, and that we were exceptional, that we would cure those on the outside, that we would change the world, that all people are equal and worthy of love, and that the concept of mental illness belongs to a system of repression. And whenever Cyryl spoke up, he talked coherently and logically, though slowly—we listened to him tensely, expecting an outburst of oddity, a sign, a stigma. When he finished, for a while silence reigned. We needed time to recover. Then gradually the ordinary chatter returned to its usual volume.

It was if nothing was actually changing. As if it could all go on and on like this, life in emergency gear; maybe a strike is the normal state of the world, the obvious one, maybe it's closest to human nature, and not that clotted, stifling order. And yet somewhere under the lining it was all becoming unbearable.

One evening Cyryl went off his head. He ran down the corridor bouncing from wall to wall, roaring terribly, inhumanly. In the sudden silence, within the stone walls of the former Gestapo HQ, on the poorly lit landings his monstrous voice thundered ominously, awaking us from the dream of casting votes, lists of demands and the idea of a rotating strike. Terrified, we clung to the walls.

B. ran after him, trying to calm him down, to take him in her arms and hug him. But he tore free. 'Cyryl, Cyryl,' she repeated steadily, as if hoping to send him to sleep. Finally he let her stop him, and she and several other people from the clinical department took him into a room. The professor of humanistic psychology told us all to disperse. So we tried to scatter down the long corridors by going into the lecture halls, where even so that dreadful roaring was still audible. I could hear dull thuds—Cyryl was banging his head against the wall.

At last they called an ambulance. Soon after we saw Cyryl being led outside in a straitjacket.

Anyone could go mad in this confinement, we commented on the event among ourselves, in these stuffy, dusty corridors thick with smoke, with the one and only view from these windows—grey blocks standing among naked trees. The ground is like army camouflage—in winter disguise, brown-and-white irregular blots. Let it end now. Let's go home.

Anna was the nearest—on Nowy Świat Street, the first gateway after the Blikle patisserie, a large courtyard, with apartment houses arranged in a broken square. A sand pit, two benches, some concrete bins, a few trees—maples and snowberry bushes. Anna's flat was on the fourth floor, high up, and that was why she was so reluctant to leave it. A passage, a living room and a kitchenette. The balcony window overlooked the street. Anna always gazed at Nowy Świat through a net curtain—she must have seen a foggy, out-of-focus street, marked by geometrical patterns. Twice a week she came downstairs, did some miserable shopping in the empty grocery, and then went to the Amatorska café for a glass of brandy. She had given up coffee long ago. I sometimes arranged to meet her there. Occasionally we sat a while at the same table as Che Guevara, but she didn't like that. She regarded his strange faces and tomfoolery with disapproval.

'Pull yourself together!' she would hiss at him.

She'd raise her glass to her lips. Only when Che had gone, mess tins jingling and cartridge cases dangling, would she say: 'It's worse than ever. I drink hot milk, I warm my feet on a hot water bottle, but even so I still can't do it. I'm awake all night, I just nod off occasionally for a quarter of an hour into strange dreams, into a languid, meaningless, agonizing doze. Oh, my child, what's to be done, what's to be done?' she would ask me dramatically, squeezing my hand in her thin fingers.

'Perhaps you haven't enough fresh air?' I would ask naively; we'd been playing this game for ages.

'Oh no, dear child, I air the place each evening for at least half an hour,' she'd reply.

'Perhaps you're eating something indigestible?' I would try again.

'No, no, dear, I eat my last meal of the day at five.'

'We can ask for some tablets,' I would eventually say.

Then she would turn away from the table and freeze in a state of total indignation.

'I could never agree to that, never,' she'd finally gasp. 'Something dreadful would happen, I don't know what, but simply dreadful.'

'Let's go for a walk, Anna.'

That was all I could suggest.

We'd cross Foksal and Copernicus Streets, then walk along Świętokrzyska Street and back to Nowy Świat. Or in the other direction, towards the river; beyond it lay enticing open spaces, which probably tempted us both, though we never spoke of it. Go through the bushes by the river, then walk along it following its endless motion, leave the city, go deep into the ice-bound fields, roam the country paths and step over boundaries marked by willow trees, maybe reach the sea, or else go the other way— south, through the mountains, and then onto a great plain. First abandon our hats, then our gloves, and finally at the edge of a vineyard leave behind our winter coats. Plunge into an ever longer day, let the light wash over us.

She shivered regardless of the weather. Chewing her lip, she would carefully inspect every yard of the pavement, the handrails, the steps, testing the kerbs with the tip of her shoe. Sometimes she'd find a hole, an imperfection, or a bit of rust, and she'd cast me a sad and knowing look. Bundled up, we'd walk along side by side.

She'd tell me to look carefully. I could see the city, always grey, in various shades of grey, unpleasant to touch, a chilly city, chapped, cracked in half, with the wound of the river down its middle. Rare buses silently glided over the bridges and came straight back. People doubled, reflecting in the large, darkened shop windows. White breath rose from their mouths, like hesitant souls. One time she asked me where I lived, and on hearing the answer Zamenhof Street, she covered her mouth in horror.

'They shouldn't have built houses on a graveyard. They should have fenced off the ruins of the ghetto from the rest of the country and made a proper graveyard, a museum. In fact, they should have done that to the entire city. They could have rebuilt Warsaw somewhere near Częstochowa, close to the Holy Virgin Mary, or on the Narew river, it's lovely there. Move out of there, dear child.'

Many times I promised her I would, and then I'd escort her back to her flat, high up, narrow, like a nesting box. I'd flick the snow off her coat, make some Madras tea in a white china teapot and put on the potatoes. She would urge me, saying: 'Talk to me, ask me some questions, tell me some stories, tire me out, let me go to sleep, I'm sure to go to sleep when you leave.'

So I would babble away. I'd tell her about the strike, about the changes that were bound to come, and about the people there, but in fact it was a strange speech. From Anna's flat the world seemed unreal, disturbing for the lack of life. There was nothing going on down there—the slogans on the banners were unreadable from this height, the noise of the demonstrations got lost in the labyrinths of courtyards, merely repeating a single tired phrase that had lost its meaning. From up here, the city consisted of roofs, antennas and chimneys—for the birds and the clouds, for the eternally overcast sky, for the darkness. Not for people.

'You see, my child, this is the end. Can you see how the image blurs at the horizon?'

'It's always like that in this sort of weather,' I reassured her.

Perhaps everyone was unwittingly taking part in a sort of cosmic war in those days. Or maybe planetary influences were grappling with each other? Yes, there must have been something going on. People were waylaying one another, shooting at each other at close range—at the pope, at Reagan, at Lennon. It looked as if any moment now the whole world would change into something completely different, as yet unidentified. Reality was in a state of flux. Illusion and disillusion were making way for each other. The veils of Maya were fluttering in the solar wind.

'I dream the world,' Anna would say, thriftily washing our cups in the sink and carefully wiping the teaspoons with a cloth. 'I dream it, but I have problems with sleep. You're not able to help me,' she would add. 'No one is. You simply come here and we talk. The world is dying, this is the end.'

I didn't believe her, but I gave up trying to bring her down to earth. Why should we all have to stand on the ground, I told myself. There's nothing wrong with thinking you keep the world in existence, you carry it on your shoulders like Atlas. That you are saving it, that you are dying for it. In a way it's true. Looking from a certain viewpoint, it's a great truth.

Anna's ontology was like this: she believed that her sleep saved the world, and that while she was sleeping the world—already spoiled, impaired, used up—regenerated. That by sleeping she was saving everything from death. No one was aware of this of course—because people are so pitifully two-dimensional ('like a sheet of paper', she would say)—only she, I and her doctor knew the truth. Even Anna's daughter, a familiar face on television, hadn't guessed it. She just took her off to hospital when the dejection and insomnia pushed Anna into months of depression.

'Why you?' I asked her at our first meeting, and she told me to cut a completed crossword into squares with letters. She made giant jigsaw puzzles out of them. After a while, she finally raised a finger enigmatically, and gesturing like John the Baptist pointed at the sky.

But how was she to save the world when she suffered from insomnia? She cast a glance to show me the people huddling in queues, the strike placards at the university—all this was happening because Anna Topiel, retired Polish language teacher and age-old resident of Nowy Świat Street, was suffering from insomnia.

As we drank the inferior Madras tea from her lovely gilded cups, she would say that the world needed about eight hours of her sleep. That wasn't very much. But, she said, she only slept for an hour, or two, restlessly, on the point of dawn. Through this feeble sleep she could hear the world creaking in its foundations. In fact the doctor had prescribed her sleeping pills and uppers, but she couldn't take them. One cannot manipulate the laws of reality with the help of primitive pharmacology. I agreed with her. I dealt the cards for whist—the dreariest card game of all, to try to cure her with boredom, to dribble calm onto her, to drag out my words, never come to the point, fan the silence, dilute the tea with water as if it were homeopathic medicine, and mumble lullabies under my breath. Those were my magic spells.

Once I saw her asleep. She was sleeping on an armchair with her head tilted to one side, and her face was calm and beautiful. Instinctively I went up to the window—I had to check. From behind low, scudding autumn clouds the sun peeped out and spilled over the roofs of the apartment houses.

* * *

On Saturday afternoon I took the tram to Che Guevara's flat, just to check up on him quickly. The strike had become rotating, tomorrow there was going to be a huge rally at the university, and there'd be a meeting this evening.

For ages he refused to open the door to me. I could hear breathing behind the door covered in newspaper, and the flutter of eyelashes at the peephole.

'Password?' he said.

I slowly uttered the first word that came into my head; I can't remember what it could have been—sky, leaf, mess tin, and then, after a brief hesitation, the lock clanked and the door opened.

He did not look good. Stripped of his bizarre props, the grenades on the belt, the helmet and the military insignia, in nothing but a grey acrylic shell-suit he seemed naked. His whole body was trembling—a gaunt, shrivelled old man—here was the whole truth about him. He wasn't a child at all, or even a frolicsome youth. He was a thin, prematurely aged old man with no childhood and no adulthood. He had gone straight from being a baby to being an old person. Now he had to make up for that lost time. Sliding in too big slippers, he led me inside his bachelor flat strewn with newspapers. The windows were curtained by old blankets, and there were towels hanging from the cornices too. His teeth were chattering with fear or cold. Steam flowed from our mouths like the speech bubbles in cartoons.

He said they'd been watching him all morning. He said first they'd done it from the street, but now they had climbed a tree and were looking through binoculars and telescopes straight into the windows. That was why he had shielded them. I wanted to ask who, who was watching him, who is out to kill you, you poor lunatic, but I didn't. I bit my tongue. Any explanation would have added to this insane vision; any word, any attempt to define his persecutor would have made the image more powerful. So I didn't respond; I set about warming up some soup that came in a bag. Shivering more and more, he watched me in the hope I would say something. I switched on an 'electric sun' heater.

'Do you want to go to hospital?' I asked him as we drank the hot soup out of mugs.

He replied that it was already too late.

'I'll go and call for help,' I said.

He raced to the door and pressed himself against it.

'Out of the question. You can't leave here. You've fallen into the trap. Any moment they'll start banging on the door.'

Indecisively I moved towards him and realized there would have to be a fight—he wouldn't let me leave.

He could read my mind. He grabbed me by the hand and squeezed. Both his and my fingers went white. In a sudden, heated impulse to panic it occurred to me that I had no idea what to do, that I must act alone, that I must become a calm and steady point of reference for this man who'd gone crazy with fear. I must take hold of his quivering, ensnare his terror and calm him down. I put a hand on his back and covered him with a blanket. I hugged him. I felt my own fear disappear like smoke. I was becoming a wide, flat plain, an immovable piece of the landscape. It's all right, I promised him, I won't leave until you want me to. I remembered Anna, the fact that she couldn't sleep and that the only salvation for the world was sleep, her sleep and ours. Only then will we recuperate, our sleep will darn all the holes through which pure evil, impenetrable darkness, gets out onto the surface.

'Sleep, Che Guevara, sleep. Let's go to sleep,' I kept saying.

Monotonously, as if reciting a special litany, I listed all the objects that were settling down to sleep—the bus stops and road signs are going to sleep, the street lamps and the steps at the entrances to shops, the cars and the chimneys on the roofs, the trees, the kerbs, the bicycles, the barriers on the bridge, the tram lines and the rubbish bins, the sweet wrappers and the dog ends, the used tickets and the empty beer bottles. And all the streets in Saska Kępa—Francuska Street, Obrońcy and Waleczni, Ateńska and Saska, and the streets in other districts too, finally whole districts of the city and whole other cities. Katowice and Gdańsk. Wałbrzych and Lublin. Białystok and Mrągowo. Sleep is gliding close to the ground, like thunder, like warm, dark smoke. It wreathes the whole country in a strange stupor. Everywhere people are raising their hands to their faces and rubbing their sleepy eyes. On the road outside Kalisz cars are stopping on the hard shoulder, and the drivers are lying down to sleep at the roadside, in the snow. Trains are stopping and dozing in the fields, ships are rocking steadily in the roadways as the port siren lulls them to sleep. The shipyards are nodding off and the assembly lines are stopping at the nocturnal factories.

The TV presenter is yawning, and is just about to lie down and sleep before the eyes of the sleepily astonished viewers.

I hugged him the way one hugs a child, and there was nothing inappropriate about it, nothing against the rules, because we were both just as tiny, just as small. We were floating in that small, paper-filled bachelor flat with its own electric sun, like a separate universe with transparent, fragile walls, a soap bubble above a large, frosty city. Slowly circling an invisible centre. I felt his body going limp and becoming heavy, as if it had ripened and were about to fall to the ground, then to gain positive strength from it that would stop him from being blown away like a sweet wrapper. It felt as if a sluice had opened between us—with a rasp, with reverence, a great river gate, and that by swaying this way we had set a powerful mechanism in motion, we had pressed a button. And now it would be impossible to stop it—the rivers were flowing into one, his and mine, coming together to unite and mingle, and for a while I had the happy feeling that this was meant to be, that I'd take on his fear and dissolve it inside myself like an ice lump in warm water, that if all this could be weighed and counted, if it were possible to measure the degree of his terror and of my serenity, it would come out to my advantage; I was larger than he was, there was more of me. My river was warmer, plumped out on the plains, heated by the sun. He was just a little stream, ice-cold and turbulent. And as soon as I had this thought, I frightened myself, because I began to lose the contours. The small stream was swelling and seething, tumbling violently, tearing up its bed. Carrying along some silt, it was going muddy, attacking with rising fury. But all this was happening underneath and couldn't be seen. Che Guevara closed his eyes and sighed. I thought he was about to fall asleep. But there underneath the fight had begun, mutual pressure, violence, invasion. Underneath this innocent old man was pushing, forcing me to breathe at his panic-stricken rate. From inside, like wheels on water, waves of panic were starting to flow towards me. Small, ice-cold splinters of it changed into trembling that gradually seized my entire body. I kept trying to get away from this terrible something, grinning and monstrous, but I knew by now there was no escape. Because this was an extreme state, a fundamental state. Everything else was just our illusion. And suddenly I realized that he, Che Guevara, was right—why hadn't it occurred to me sooner?—they were watching us, sitting in a tree, preparing the worst torture chambers, they knew all about us. Some foggy people, dark figures knitted out of shadow, but joined by slimy umbilical cords to the dark centre of the earth. Yes, why shouldn't they be sitting in the trees, when after all, we knew they were capable of anything? Why wouldn't they be watching us through binoculars from the poplar outside the window? How could that have seemed absurd to me? Dozens of men in dark dustcoats slipping down alleys; militia vans hidden in courtyards; the quiet crackling of a radio station; the eyes on stalks of night-vision devices aimed at every window. At their secret headquarters they have tons of equipment we could never imagine. They keep a hand on the pulse of each one of us. They conduct history, they pull on strings, they brainwash us, they tell us to see what they want—and that's what we see. They stick ready-made opinions under our noses—and we repeat them. They print fake newspapers in which they describe the world the way they want it to be. They force us to believe in something that doesn't exist and to deny the obvious. And we do it. They impersonate our friends, and even—yes, yes—I can never be sure if the person I see in the mirror is really me.

I broke free, adjusted the curtains made of towels, and just in case I turned off the main gas tap. I tiptoed to the door to check it was locked and bolted. He followed me with the gaze of someone who knows.

'You see? You see? Didn't I say? Didn't I?' he muttered.

There we sat until morning on a bed made of newspapers, huddled close. All night strange ideas bloomed in my head, like those nondescript white plants that grow on windowpanes on frosty nights. I rubbed them out, but they kept on growing, though more feebly by the hour. Maybe the approaching dawn was chasing them away. Finally I must have fallen asleep, because I was awoken by his voice and the gurgling of water in the kettle.

He was standing by the gas stove attaching an empty cardboard holster to his belt. The curtains were off now, and metallic winter light was falling through the windows.

'It's all over,' he said. 'They've gone. But they'll be back.'

I was stunned, as if I'd smoked a packet of cigarettes, as if I'd fainted and been brought round. With disbelief I inspected the flat. Suspiciously I examined the branches of the trees. I read the headlines of the newspapers scattered all over the place. I've had a panic attack, I've had a psychotic episode, I thought. He's infected me, I let myself be infected, he hypnotized me, I gave in to suggestion.

'Che, you're going to hospital. I'll go and make the call.'

He didn't protest, and began to collect his things. When I went outside, my thoughts slowly returned to normal, shaking themselves down like wet dogs. They came together and hastened onto parade. They lined up in ranks and fell into formation. They started to number off in turn. The streets were deserted, but it was a Sunday. Today was the rally. Ambulance service number. Anna—call her and ask if by chance she slept well last night.

I went into a phone booth and dialled the number several times, but the phone must have been out of order. Not a single tram came by. I walked across the bridge to the other side of the city, until on Jerozolimskie Avenue I saw a cavalcade of armoured cars go rumbling by.

Return of the Evil One (2011)

Krzysztof Varga

Patryk woke up on a bench at Three Crosses Square with his head exploding into a thousand pieces; by turns it felt as huge and heavy as a medicine ball and then as tiny as a ping-pong ball, and his brain was like a hard little nut, bouncing off its inner walls. He felt as if someone were forcibly pushing his eyes deep into his skull, causing pain that filled not just his eye sockets, but radiated throughout his body. Large black spots swirled before these wretched eyes, and when he made the effort to stand up, keeping his legs wide apart for balance, his inner ear went haywire. As he tried to stay upright, he swayed dangerously, grabbing at non-existent supports. He sat down again and closed his eyes, thinking that in the first place he should go to a pharmacy and buy some aspirin, then drink a cold beer, which always helps in these situations, or alternatively he should drink a beer and then buy aspirin. On the other side of the square, behind St Alexander's church, there were some trendy bars, open round the clock; he'd have a beer there, maybe a coffee too, and thus make a start on the arduous course of treatment that would help him to return to the land of the living, because right now he felt like a zombie, only alive in that he could move and think, but otherwise dead.

He slowly opened his eyes, afraid that if he did it too fast he'd be thrown off balance again, though now he was sitting, rather than trying to stand up, gripping the bench with both hands. At first all he could see was a large black blot, but gradually, as his pupils got used to the light, the image began to acquire shapes and distinct contours, and yet there was something extremely disturbing about it. The shape of Three Crosses Square was familiar, but different somehow, and the people walking past him were not the types he usually saw on the streets of Warsaw; their clothes were different and, he noticed to his consternation, as they walked past him, they were overtly, if not ostentatiously staring at him, showing the sort of amazement and curiosity with which one stares at a weirdo. But the strangest thing of all was that the whole scene was in black and white: the square, the houses surrounding it, and the leaves on the trees, which ought to be green, were all a shade of grey, like a washed-out black T-shirt that's been worn in the sunshine. Instead of the usual red-and-yellow livery of the city transport the bus that was just pulling up at the stop outside the Deaf-and-Dumb Institute was entirely black, with only a few white details. Even more surprisingly, the vehicle was of a make that wasn't used in Warsaw, and if it ever had been, it was a very long time ago, at least fifty years earlier. All this was shocking, so he closed his eyes again and wondered feverishly, while sweating like a pig, what on earth was going on. 'Something must have happened to my brain during yesterday's high jinks,' he thought, 'I must have damaged my pituitary gland or my hippocampus, I must have overdone the fun and games in those clubs in the Praga district, and then finished myself off in Powiśle, so now something has changed for good in my head—I must have damaged the nerves that control vision if I'm seeing everything in black and white, and if familiar shapes are distorted like in a bad dream.' He opened his eyes and looked around in horror. Nothing had changed since his previous inspection of his surroundings, everything was still black and white, the passing buses looked like a parade of antiques out of a transport museum, and the people seemed to have come from the old film chronicles they used to show at the cinema before the main feature in the days before advertising.

Their clothes were grey-and-brown, the men were in rain-coats, carrying leather briefcases, and some of them wore berets, while the women had strange hairdos, including lots of buns, though many of them were hiding their hair under headscarves. These were not the sort of women you encountered in Warsaw any more, though perhaps you might see them somewhere in the provinces—women who worked in grocery stores, prematurely aged by the cares of daily life, might have those hairdos and clothes, but not the women on Three Crosses Square!

The people passing him were still staring at him with a curiosity he had never experienced in Warsaw before, though he looked normal, he was dressed normally, tidily, if not fashionably, though not flashily; after all, hanging out at trendy bars did demand the appropriate look. Now he realized that although his appearance could be described as normal or average, he did look completely different from all the passers-by who were casting judgemental glances at him. He was wearing a pair of white trainers, jeans, and a motley T-shirt under a denim jacket; the messy haircut he had procured for himself yesterday at a salon called 'The Hair Gallery' was extremely different from those sported by the residents of this strange black-and-white Warsaw, to whom he must have looked quite like an alien.

'Hey, Gienek,' he suddenly heard a young man say, which meant that although he had lost his ability to see the world in colour, he hadn't lost his hearing. 'Take a peek at that monkey over there.'

He looked in the direction from where this slightly screechy voice was coming, and saw some young men in badly-cut cropped jackets, slightly too narrow trousers and flat caps. The one who had spoken was pointing at him, and his narrow, bird-like face, speckled with weeping, adolescent acne, twisted into an unsympathetic grimace that was presumably supposed to be a sort of disdainful smirk.

'Hey, creep,' said a second member of the group, a pale lad with grotesquely protruding ears, 'gissa fag.'

His tone carried a threat rather than a request, and Patryk realized that trouble was brewing. He didn't have any cigarettes, and even if he smoked and had some, these young hooligans, who looked like the teddy boys he'd once seen in some old photos, wouldn't be satisfied with this tribute and weren't going to go away quietly. They were clearly looking for a fight, probably bored with aimlessly trailing about the city.

'You gone deaf, fancy boy? Don't you know Polish?' said the first one, who had pointed at him earlier. 'Give us a fag and a couple of zlots for some booze if you wanna get home with your bonce in one piece. Or back to the circus you've escaped from.' He laughed in a surprisingly shrill tone, and the rest of the company—including Jug Ears and

202 ■ Krzysztof Varga

a gnome-like, squat blond boy, silent until now, at first glance strong with a flushed pink face—cackled along with him.

Patryk realized that although they were so amused, they were definitely not joking, and if they wanted to have some fun it would be at his expense. He looked around, but all the people who had been walking past moments before, staring at him so closely, had as if on command boarded buses or run down Konopnicka Street or Wiejska to see to urgent business. The only person watching the development of events was the newspaper-kiosk man, who was leaning out of his little window, or rather his bushy grey moustache was leaning out of it, yet above that moustache there was undoubtedly a pair of eyes carefully scouring the vicinity.

'I haven't got any cigarettes or money,' said Patryk in a slightly trembling voice, feeling his heart begin to beat faster and louder, and his hands to sweat, as if he had only just removed them from viscous, greasy liquid. In any case, part of what he said was the truth. Part of it, because he really didn't smoke and had no cigarettes, but yes, in fact he did have some money, though not much, probably only about twenty zlotys after last night's shenanigans; naturally he did have his credit and debit cards on him, but he doubted that these young men, who had just surrounded him in a tight semi-circle, had brought card payment terminals with them.

'Look at that, he even knows how to talk Polish,' said Jug Ears in amazement, leaning back and sticking his hands deeper in his pockets, which must have been to demonstrate his aggressive disdain for the stranger; getting impatient with all the lengthy foreplay, the gnome added: 'Let's cut the crap, let's just beat him up and get out of here, Gienek, 'cos I've got an awful thirst.'

'Don't forget, Fatso, we've still got to report at Mr Kruszyna's today, because there's gonna be a job for us this evening, so no drinking,' Jug Ears scolded him, and the gnome called Fatso saddened noticeably, casting Patryk hateful looks as if he were to blame for the fact that for now he must lay off the booze. He came up to Patryk, and as he moved forwards, so did Jug Ears and Spotty, tightening the circle. Jug Ears took an elongated object from his pocket and made a swift motion with his thumb; a silver steel blade flashed before Patryk's eyes, as to his horror he realized it was a flick knife.

'Hand over the loot, you sucker, or your own Vater won't recognize you,' Jug Ears muttered menacingly through his teeth, and the mocking smirks faded from the hooligans' faces like water flowing down a windowpane. Now their horrible, ugly mugs looked really dangerous, and with a shaking hand Patryk began to rummage in his inside jacket pocket, where he kept his wallet. He was even ready to hand over his credit cards and give them the PIN numbers, anything to be left in peace, anything for Jug Ears to put away his flick knife and be gone, but just then the knife blade swished before his eyes like a final warning.

'All right, wait a moment,' he muttered because his teeth were chattering with fear. He took out his wallet, discreetly looking around in case the police were somewhere nearby, just in case a police car happened to be passing, then he could throw himself to one side in desperation, avoiding the knife blade, and run off, calling for help. Unfortunately there were no policemen in sight, and all the passers-by had vanished as if a sudden epidemic had wiped them out. He took out his last two bank notes, a twenty and a fifty; he was surprised he had that much money left after last night's taxi rides and all the expensive drinks in trendy clubs. Unable to stop shaking, he gave them to Jug Ears, who took them with his left hand, because in his right he was still holding the flick knife, though now he was hiding it discreetly in his palm, with the dexterity of a circus performer.

Jug Ears glanced at the bank notes, frowned, and hissed: 'What sort of a pathetic joke is this, loser? What's this? Money? A pink Bolesław the Brave? A blue Kazimierz the Great? Drew them yourself, you creep? They've come out pretty neat, but this isn't real money, there should be a worker woman and a fisherman, and it should say Polish People's Republic, our socialist homeland. We'll take you straight to the cop shop as a morally suspect figure who's trying to put fake money into circulation and conducting subversive activity. We'll be doing the people's government a service, won't we, gang?' He bared his crooked teeth, going black for lack of oral hygiene and too much nicotine, and Fatso and Spotty cackled in solidarity.

Patryk was trembling; it was the first time anything like this had ever happened to him, no one had ever attacked him before, demanded money or threatened him with a knife, least of all in broad daylight in one of Warsaw's main squares. He had always avoided unsafe places, he always took cabs to the bars on Ząbkowska Street and 11 November Street, and he never went home by night bus, but who could have predicted that something like this would happen to him on Three Crosses Square? Feeling a painful, shameful pressure on his bladder, he had a violent need to urinate, and was terrified he was about to compromise himself by pissing in his pants. The smiles had vanished from his attackers' faces, giving way to angry scowls, and suddenly the gnome called Fatso aimed a straight right at Patryk's head, at lightning speed and with professional skill, a perfect blow, no doubt observed at boxing matches at the Gwardia club, and worthy of Zygmunt Chychła, the champion himself. Patryk went flying backwards and rolled onto the ground, as sudden darkness exploded before his eyes. But it only lasted a moment, because he soon got up,

determined to make his getaway, to anywhere at all, towards
Nowy Świat Street or in the entirely opposite direction,
southwards, he'd run off shouting 'Help!'—then they'd be
sure to leave him alone, they wouldn't dare chase him so
brazenly, at most only their angry insults would catch up
with him. He was just starting to get to his feet when suddenly something extraordinary happened: in the spot
where his attackers had been standing seconds earlier there
was a terrible kerfuffle; he could see some figures swishing
through the air, but it was impossible to tell exactly what
was going on; only brief shouts emerged from the tumult:
'Jesus!', 'Christ!' And suddenly it was all over, as fast as it
had begun, and there lay his three oppressors, knocked to
the ground. Fatso was in an embryonic position, with his
knees drawn up almost to his chin, holding his belly and
moaning incomprehensibly, Spotty was on his back, uncon-
scious, with his arms thrown wide like a criminal crucified
on the pavement, and only Jug Ears was trying to stand up,
but hadn't the strength to do more than kneel, bent forwards, with his face in his hands as he repeated 'Oh God!
Mother!' A stream, rather than a dribble of blood trickled
from between his fingers as he pressed them to his ugly
face. Patryk was dumbstruck, and stared in stupefaction at
the hooligans who had seemed so dangerous, but who'd
been beaten up and eliminated from the fight; in less than
twenty seconds someone had knocked them all out in the

first round. He didn't know who had done it, but suddenly opposite his eyes another pair of eyes appeared, extremely unlike any he had ever seen before; these eyes were large and shining, but shining with the whiteness of snow! They only appeared for a moment and instantly vanished. 'Jesus, where do I know them from?' said Patryk to himself. 'White eyes, where have I seen them? No, I've never seen them, I've read about them somewhere, Jesus, where was it?'

Suddenly he pulled himself together, looked around and saw a medium-sized figure in a light raincoat, swiftly making off towards Wiejska Street. He leaped up and went in violent pursuit of it—of the man with the shocking white eyes. The three young thugs were still lying there, moaning and groaning. All of a sudden the surrounding area was swarming with people. Patryk heard shouts behind him: 'Bandits! They're attacking young people in broad daylight! Catch them! That fellow over there beat them up!' Two militiamen ran up from the direction of Książęca Street, one holding onto his cap with his left hand, and the other blowing into a whistle as hard as he could.

The man in the raincoat ran down Wiejska Street towards the Parliament building, and Patryk raced after him, though there were black spots exploding before his eyes and his lungs were trying to tear free of his ribcage. He was still seeing everything in black and white, as if watching a movie on a very old television, but he had got used to it by now; what mattered most was to catch up with the man who had dealt with the bandits so speedily, and had probably saved his life. It never occurred to Patryk that his mysterious defender might do the same thing to him as Fatso, Jug Ears and Spotty; all he could think about was where he knew the man from, because he was sure he recognized him, though he had never met him before in person. Suddenly the man disappeared from sight and Patryk put on the brakes, disoriented. The sound of the militia whistle had stopped, and he couldn't hear any shouts either, so no one had chased after them from Three Crosses Square; evidently the militiamen were occupied with writing down the statements of witnesses of the attack and the victims of the beating, sparing themselves a dangerous pursuit. Patryk stood looking around hesitantly, amid the strange black-and-white silence. Unexpectedly he felt a tug at his arm and a strong force pulled him into a gateway. Before he'd had time to let out a shriek of horror, he felt a rough hand gagging his mouth, and he heard a loud whisper: 'Keep quiet! I won't do you any harm, but don't shout.'

He nodded to show that he understood and accepted the terms of capitulation. The hand unstuck from his mouth and ran the length of the raincoat, as the disgusted attacker wiped it clean of Patryk's spittle. In the gloom of the gateway to a house that was still a post-war ruin they couldn't be seen at all, so no passer-by would have noticed that any suspicious figures were lurking there.

'Why did you run after me? Do you want to get me and yourself into trouble?' asked the man in that strange, loud whisper. 'If you wanted to escape you could have gone down Konopnicka Street to the park and on to Solec—they'd never have found you there, but you had to run after me,' he added reproachfully.

'I wanted to thank you,' said Patryk, who had just had a brainwave. Swallowing thick saliva through his suddenly strangely constricted throat, he added boldly: 'Mr Nowak...'

For a while there was an ominous silence, until finally, paralysed like a rabbit being stared at by a snake, Patryk heard a remark uttered not in a whisper any more but in a nasty, rasping voice: 'How do you know my name? I don't recall having met you before...'

'Your name is Henryk Nowak,' said Patryk. 'You're the hero of this city, the militia are after you, Lieutenant Dziarski from police HQ has got it in for you, and has set himself the task of catching you as a point of honour, but I think on the quiet he's on your side,' he said quite freely now, having entirely forgotten that he had only just got away with his life, and had also come close to being arrested; by now he had even forgotten that he was seeing the world in black and white, that everything around him looked like a very old film chronicle, that the trolleybus he had just seen rolling down Piękna Street looked like a large, clumsy may-bug, and that not even that had surprised him, even though trolleybuses hadn't existed in Warsaw for several decades. That's to say they still ran in the 1990s, he could remember the one and only line 51 from the South Station to Piaseczno, but there hadn't been any in the city centre for almost forty years; he wasn't even born then. 'I'm still young,' thought Patryk with self-satisfaction.

The man was silent, probably making an intense mental effort—how on earth did this strange-looking boy know his name, how did he know about Dziarski, and generally where had he sprung from in this city in such a strange costume and hairstyle? Not even the most extreme teddy boys looked like that. He was amazed, wondering at the same time if he had done the right thing by rescuing him from the hooligans; the deed might have unpleasant consequences for him, because this oddball knew a bit too much, he even knew his name. Meanwhile Patryk excitedly carried on:

'Not just Dziarski is on your side, but the whole city is behind you, editor Kolanko from the Evening Express, Dr Halski, and all the ordinary citizens,' he continued, but Henryk Nowak cut him short with a remark as sharp as a butcher's knife: 'Not all!'

'Well, yes,' reflected Patryk, 'that's right, Chairman Merino isn't on your side, nor is the boxer Kruszyna or Jerzy Meteor, because you cause them trouble.'

'Merino is no Merino,' said Henryk Nowak, and it occurred to Patryk that for the city's legendary superhero he had a disappointingly banal name—among all those characters called things like Merino, Meteor, Kalodont and Kompot, the name Nowak, of which there must have been thousands in this city, sounded commonplace.

'Since you know my name, I'd like to know yours,' added Henryk Nowak, drilling his gaze into Patryk; his expression was menacing and firm. 'What's your name and where's your pad? Probably not in Warsaw because no one wears clothes like those here,' he added with distaste.

'I'm Patryk Milusiński and I live in Kabaty,' said Patryk with a note of unjustified pride in his voice.

'So where's this Kabaty?' asked Nowak in the tone of an interrogator. 'What part of Poland?'

'In Warsaw,' replied Patryk, amazed by his saviour's ignorance. 'It's the last stop on the metro,' he added, instantly reflecting that in the Warsaw where he had ended up, where Henryk Nowak meted out justice to ordinary street hoodlums, petty crooks, pickpockets and serious drunks, there was no metro yet. 'I mean, where the metro station will be one day, that's to say, er...from your perspective, because, er...how can I put it?'

'Normally: briefly and to the point, because I understand less and less of this, and I haven't the time or the desire to stand here in this gateway with a layabout like you. I've got a lot of things to do, I'm gonna split soon, so don't kid me around, just tell it like at holy confession.' There was rising impatience and irritation in Nowak's voice.

'So you see, I was born in 1975, I live in Kabaty which they started to build in the 1990s, the place where the metro goes to now, they spent twenty-five years building it and there's only one line, but you can go all the way to Huta Warszawa on it, I was there yesterday at a couple of clubs and something happened to my head, and suddenly I woke up on Three Crosses Square, but not the one I know, just the one from fifty-five years ago, without the trendy bars, without anything I know at all, and then those hooligans attacked me and you rescued me, and I know you're Henryk Nowak because I've read a novel about you, I know everything, I know who's who, I can tell you everything about the ticket scam Merino's planning for the Poland–Hungary match, and that then he wants to escape the country with Olimpia Szuwar, I know what scores you have to settle with him, and I know who Citizen Shaggy is, I know he's not really the ringleader but a common vagrant whose legend was made up by Merino, because he's the one who runs everything in this city, I know everything—now do you believe me?'

'You're lying,' said Nowak, and his voice was more like the hiss of a snake than human speech, 'and I don't like lies. Don't play the tough guy because I don't like tough guys who tell lies.'

To his horror, Patryk saw that Nowak's eyes were flashing again, and they were dazzlingly white, even whiter and more terrifying in the dense darkness of the gateway. Before he could say that he wasn't lying at all, that he always spoke the truth, and that what he had said just now was as true as could be, a right hook landed on his jaw at lighting speed. As Patryk slid down the wall, his eyes sank deep into his skull, and everything around him went dark; in this darkness even Henryk Nowak's white eyes disappeared, and Patryk felt himself falling into a bottomless black well.

When he came round, once again he had a dreadful headache, as if his brain were exploding into a thousand pieces. He rubbed his jaw and confirmed to his relief that it was intact. Leaning against the wall, he struggled to his feet; this time red spots danced before his eyes, and he feared he was about to lose consciousness. But after a while the spots vanished and, breathing heavily, Patryk rolled out of the gateway into Wiejska Street. The sudden brightness assailed him, and he closed his eyes. When he opened them again something astonished him, though in the first instance he couldn't understand what. But then it dawned on him: the scene around him was in colour—the leaves on the trees were green, the body of a passing car was blue, and the kiosk opposite shimmered with hundreds of intensely colourful magazine covers. Disoriented, he headed for Three Crosses Square. Once he reached it, he felt that from watching black-and-white TV he had suddenly switched to watching light entertainment on a vast plasma screen. Over on the left once again he saw the statue of Wincenty Witos, just as in the past, with some youths in peaked caps practising stunts on their skateboards underneath it. One after another, red-and-yellow buses with orange display screens drove up to the stop. He boarded one that was heading for Nowy Świat Street, but at the roundabout it turned left into Jerozolimskie Avenue, towards the Centrum metro station. Patryk stood next to the driver's cabin and gazed out of the front window. They were approaching the roundabout featuring the big artificial palm tree that had always annoyed him, but now as it came into sight he felt a sort of affection for it, and at last, for the first time in ages, he breathed a deep sigh of relief.

Notes on the Authors and Stories, with Suggestions for Further Reading

Bolesław Prus (1847–1912) 'Apparitions' was written in 1911, when Poland was still partitioned among the neighbouring empires, and Warsaw was, technically speaking, a Russian city. Throughout their national captivity, the Poles fought against the Russian occupation relentlessly, leading in many cases to tragic death or Siberian exile. As a teenager, Bolesław Prus had taken part in the 1863 Uprising against the Russians, and was wounded, arrested, imprisoned, and very nearly exiled. He died too soon to see the restoration of an independent Poland after the First World War. In 'Apparitions' the fate of noblemen from the countries occupied by Russia is reflected in their conversation and names ('Heave-sigh-lo', 'Post-exile-ski'). It is set in the picturesque Old Town Marketplace (or 'Rynek' in Polish), probably the first port of call for any tourist visiting Warsaw, though today's Marketplace is a reconstruction following the devastation of the Second World War. Prus's optimistic vision of the future is uncanny; though Warsaw is not exactly 'Paradise Regained', nowadays there are indeed museums and tourists on the square, and Fukier's wineshop is still there. (NB: Prejudice against the Jews as a lower social caste was unfortunately widespread in the historical past, and is reflected in this story.)

Bolesław Prus is the archetypal Warsaw writer; he started his career as a journalist, writing 'Weekly Chronicles' that are a valuable record of everyday life in Warsaw in the latter part of the nineteenth century. When he progressed to fiction in the 1880s, his first short stories were about the indigent tenants of a Warsaw apartment building. But he is best known for his novels, the most famous of which is *The Doll* (1890), regarded by Czesław Miłosz as the greatest example of Polish realism, the embodiment of Polish nineteenth-century society, which Prus exposes as lamentably inert and hopeless. Mostly set in Warsaw, the story features many identifiable locations (not all extant), including the building on Krakowskie Przedmieście where the central character, Stanisław Wokulski, lives and works. *The Doll* is available in English translation, by David Welsh and Anna Zaranko, published by New York Review Books.

Maria Kuncewiczowa (1899–1989) 'ZOO'—reportage rather than a short story, though Maria Kuncewiczowa wrote fiction as well as diaries—was first written for a newspaper column, and later appeared in a book titled *The Warsaw Stagecoach*, a collection of sketches reflecting the atmosphere of the large, busy city. It was originally published in 1935, and thus in the interwar period from 1918 to 1939, when Poland was once again an independent country for the first time since 1795 (when the neighbouring empires wiped it off the map). Warsaw's zoo, on the eastern bank of the river Vistula in the working-class Praga district, was opened in 1928 and still functions on the same site. Kuncewiczowa observes not just the caged animals, but the people visiting the zoo with the same comical and mildly cynical eye, painting a picture of Warsaw at a time when the whole city was soon to be turned upside down, if not blown apart, in the Second World War. The zoo itself was a significant site during the Nazi occupation, when its heroic director Jan Żabiński and his wife Antonina sheltered Jewish refugees within its large grounds. Many of the animals were killed by the Nazis, and the zoo suffered bombardments. Antonina Żabińska's own book about the zoo and their wartime activities inspired Diane Ackerman's book, *The Zookeeper's Wife*, which was made into a successful American film in 2017.

Maria Kuncewiczowa was one of the best female novelists to emerge in the Second Republic, as independent Poland was known from 1918 to 1939. Her short stories and novels soon established her as a writer in the 'Western' style, focusing on human psychology rather than political commitments. To escape the war, in 1940 she moved to England, and then in 1955 to the USA, where she taught at the University of Chicago. In 1970 she returned to Poland for the rest of her life, though she wintered in Italy.

Readers wishing to explore Polish literature in more depth are encouraged to read *The Modern Polish Mind*, a superb anthology of stories and essays compiled by Maria Kuncewiczowa, published in 1963 by Grosset & Dunlap.

Jarosław Iwaszkiewicz (1894–1980) Jarosław Iwaszkiewicz was a poet, novelist, and prolific author of short stories. Written in 1945, 'Icarus' is set at the heart of Warsaw, on the elegant street named Krakowskie Przedmieście (literally 'Krakow Foretown'), part of the Royal Route that links the Old Town and the Royal Castle, and the location for Warsaw University, the Presidential Palace, and several splendid churches and grand hotels. Throughout the Second World War, Warsaw was occupied by the Nazis, who created a persistently threatening and tense atmosphere, and carried out frequent round-ups, in which random Polish civilians were arrested and either sent to camps or prisons, forced to do slave labour, or summarily executed.

During the war, Iwaszkiewicz hid many Jews and other endangered people at his house outside the city, a meeting place for various intellectuals engaged in the underground movement. The sinister incident described in this story is all too true to life. Iwaszkiewicz grew up in Ukraine, and migrated to Warsaw in 1918, where he was soon established as a poet, though he gained wider public popularity through his novels, novellas and short stories, opera librettos and plays. One of his most famous works is *Mother Joan of the Angels*, about the seventeenth-century French convent at Loudun where the nuns were possessed by devils; it was made into a memorable film by Jerzy Kawalerowicz. After the war he was a leading literary figure in People's Poland, and as president of the Writer's Union was frowned upon by some for cooperating with the communist authorities, though in fact he often helped other writers who were having difficulties with them.

More of his work can be found in English translation in *The Birch Grove and Other Stories*, translated by Antonia Lloyd-Jones and published by CEU Press Classics (2002).

Ludwik Hering (1908–1984) During the Second World War, the painter, actor, and writer Ludwik Hering lived in occupied Warsaw. From the Aryan side, he witnessed the fate of the Jews forced to live in appalling conditions within the confines of the ghetto until they were deported to death camps. He wrote three short stories about it, 'Meta', 'Traces', and 'The Greengrocer's', more literary reportage rather than fiction, documenting the terrible truth that the outside world either had ignored or was powerless to combat.

During the occupation, Ludwik Hering worked as a watchman at a tannery and was actively involved in helping Jews to escape from the ghetto and find refuge. After a series of tribulations of his own at the hands of the Soviet 'liberators', he survived the war, and with his niece Ludmiła Murawska and his good friend Miron Białoszewski founded an exceptional three-person theatre company, Teatr Osobny (The Independent Theatre), which performed plays by Białoszewski at his apartment. Hering also wrote some of the plays, and the company made their own costumes and scenery. Miron Białoszewski was famous as a poet, and as the author of non-fiction describing everyday life in detail, including most famously his superb *Memoir of the Warsaw Uprising*, which was translated into English by Madeline G. Levine and is available from New York Review Books.

At the heart of what was once the ghetto area, POLIN—the Museum of the History of Polish Jews—now attracts visitors from the world over, and commemorates the life, rather than the death, of Poland's Jews.

Zofia Petersowa (1899 or 1902–1955) Zofia Petersowa made her living as a literary translator (from German and Russian), journalist, and prison worker running a home for prisoners' children and a penal facility for girls. Her journalism includes a vivid account of the Warsaw Uprising, and she also wrote a collection of short stories based on her wartime experiences, *Revenge: Tales of the Occupation* (1947), from which 'The Funeral' is taken. Her husband died in a German prison camp during the war, and after it she worked at a publishing house and for Polish Radio. This story is set immediately before and after the Warsaw Uprising, in which the Poles staged a desperate final attempt to stand up to the Germans, but failed dramatically; the Germans' final act before being driven out by the Soviet Red Army was to blow up most of the city, leaving it in ruins.

Many Polish authors wrote fiction that acts as documentary evidence of Warsaw's suffering during the Second World War. Apart from Białoszewski's above-mentioned memoir, little is available in English translation, but Andrzej Wajda's excellent film, *Kanał* ('The Sewer') is based on a short story by Jerzy Stefan Stawiński. Zofia Nałkowska's diaries provide an excellent record of life in Nazi-occupied Warsaw, but have yet to be translated, though *Medallions*, her collected stories about Nazi atrocities resulting from her work for a committee investigating war crimes, has been translated by Diana Kuprel and published by Northwestern University Press (2000).

Marek Hłasko (1934–1969) Marymont is a suburb in the north of Warsaw, nowadays the site of several housing developments. 'First Step in the Clouds' is set there in 1955, when it was a typical residential area with the 'Family Allotment Gardens' that are a major feature of many Polish cities. These gardens within the city have a whole life and culture of their own, as a place where the citizens can not only grow vegetables and flowers, but also relax in the summer, or even stay overnight in the wooden cabins that are a feature of almost every allotment.

Often labelled as Poland's 'angry young man', Marek Hłasko wrote hard-hitting novels and stories that featured jaded lower-class heroes disappointed by life, and passionate but doomed love affairs. He grew up in wartime Warsaw, and ascribed his literary obsession with violent death and catastrophe to his early experiences of hunger and terror. But his work is not without humour and has enduring appeal; several of his novels have been published in English translation, including *Beautiful Twentysomethings*, translated by Ross Ufberg for Northern Illinois University Press (2013), a wryly comical autobiography that describes Hłasko's relationships with celebrities including Roman Polański, how he exploited his resemblance to James Dean, and how his writing caused him to be exiled from Poland at the age of 28. He died at the age of 35, probably as the result of an accidental overdose.

Kazimierz Orłoś (b. 1935) Kazimierz Orłoś is a novelist, screenwriter and dramatist. As a small boy, he was almost executed during the Warsaw Uprising. 'The Palace of Culture', first written in 1957 and thus at the start of his career, shows the critical attitude that would later get him into trouble with the communist censors. Throughout that era he bravely stood up against abuses of human rights by the authorities.

Following the devastation of the Second World War, Warsaw was gradually rebuilt, but as the country was now run by a communist government under Soviet control, that influence was reflected in some of the city's new architecture. When the Palace of Culture and Science was built in 1955, it was the eighth tallest building in the world, and is still Warsaw's second highest, despite the cluster of skyscrapers that have joined it in the past thirty years. Originally named after Joseph Stalin, the Soviet tyrant's infamous gift to the Polish nation dominated the Warsaw skyline, a constant reminder that Big Brother was watching. Similar to the seven 'wedding cake' buildings that characterize Moscow, the Palace houses cinemas, theatres, university departments, the offices of various state-run organizations, a number of radio stations, two museums, and a swimming pool. Some still see it as a negative memento of the communist era and want it to be demolished, but it is so familiar by now that it has taken on a cult status.

The Palace of Culture has inspired several works of non-fiction and also features in pop culture, in cinema, and in fiction, most notably in the surreal novel *A Minor Apocalypse* by Tadeusz Konwicki, in which the narrator is tasked with setting himself alight in front of the Palace of Culture as a form of political protest, and roams around central Warsaw carrying a can of petrol; his wanderings take him up to the viewing gallery at the top of the Palace. Translated by Richard Lourie, it was most recently published in English by Dalkey Archive Press in 2009.

Hanna Krall (b. 1935) Hanna Krall is one of Poland's leading authors of reportage. Although her stories are entirely true, they often read like fiction. As a child, she was the only member of her immediate family to survive the Holocaust thanks to the efforts of non-Jewish Poles who kept her hidden. Her internationally best-known book is *Shielding the Flame*, about the Warsaw Ghetto Uprising leader and sole survivor, Marek Edelman (translated by Joanna Stasińska and Lawrence Weschler, published by Henry Holt & Co, 1986).

The facts described in 'The Presence' (written in 1997) could only have taken place in the Muranów district where the Jewish ghetto once stood, until the Nazis deported its residents to death camps and razed the buildings to the ground. The area can never forget its wartime past, and it is hard not to feel a sense of tragedy and absence in the air. Recently, mirabelle plum trees, allegedly grown from plum stones taken to safety in America by refugees, have been planted in the district again.

As mentioned earlier, at the heart of this area visitors can find POLIN—the Museum of the History of Polish Jews—a superb commemoration of Jewish life in Poland. Available in English, *In the Garden of Memory* by Joanna Olczak-Ronikier is a recent family memoir that explains the place of Polish Jews within Warsaw society before the war (translated by Antonia Lloyd-Jones and published by Weidenfeld & Nicolson, 2005). The author also includes her own childhood experiences of surviving the Holocaust, when she was hidden by nuns in a Warsaw convent.

Antoni Libera (b. 1949) Stage director, novelist, and translator, Antoni Libera lives in the northern district of Żoliborz, a leafy residential suburb full of fine modernist architecture built between the wars. 'The View from Above and Below' is Libera's paean to the area, and features many buildings that are still there—notably the Tęcza (Rainbow) Cinema and the boiler house, which is now the Kotłownia restaurant, on Suzin Street. The story also describes the city centre streets where Libera—like the hero of the story—spent his own childhood. Many of these places had their names changed in the communist era, but since the restoration of democracy in 1989, now have their original names again. Thus, the city's past and present are connected, as in this story, showing Warsaw's essential continuity despite the terrible upheaval of the Second World War.

Antoni Libera is famous in Poland as translator and director of the plays of Samuel Beckett, who referred to Libera as 'my ambassador in Eastern Europe'. He is also the author of the humorous novel *Madame*, set in the communist-dominated Warsaw of his own teenage years in the early 1970s. The narrator is a precocious school student whose obsession with his French teacher inspires his intellectual pursuits, many of which are frustrated by the limitations of the dismal communist era. Translated into English by Agnieszka Kołakowska, it was published by Canongate in 2004.

Zbigniew Mentzel (b. 1951) Warsaw may be the only capital city where the banks of the river that flows through it are still lined with woods and beaches. In summer the Varsovians swim in the river Vistula and sunbathe beside it. A lifelong resident of Warsaw, novelist, essayist, and journalist Zbigniew Mentzel often expresses ironical nostalgia for the communist era of his youth. In this autobiographical sketch written in 2001 he describes some surprising aspects of Warsaw in that era, including the joys of angling in the river, and—as in the story by Kazimierz Orłoś—his own experience of failing to see the view from the Palace of Culture. The creepy image of the insurgents who were walled into the bridge is another instance of Warsaw's historical past never letting itself be forgotten, but remaining to haunt the present.

The Vistula has strong symbolism in Poland as its longest river, running from the mountains in the south through

Kraków, the country's historic capital and most picturesque city, through Warsaw, all the way to Gdańsk on the northern coast, where it emerges into the Baltic Sea. Inevitably it turns up in art, music, and literature. In Janusz Korczak's 1934 children's novel, *Kaytek the Wizard*, the hero's favourite place of refuge is the Vistula riverbank; he uses his magical powers to conjure up an island in the middle of the river, with a castle on it, though his dream home is soon destroyed. Mostly set in Warsaw, the novel features many city landmarks, and was published in English translation by Antonia Lloyd-Jones in 2012 (Penlight Publications).

Olga Tokarczuk (b. 1962) In 'Che Guevara' Olga Tokarczuk is inspired by her experience as a student of clinical psychology at Warsaw University in the early 1980s. Her student career coincided with the era of Solidarity, the heady months when all over Poland a revolution was going on in defiance of the communist government. In a nationwide wave of protest, factory after factory, and profession after profession, staged strikes to fight for better social, political, and economic conditions. The students were no exception, as the story shows, holding sit-in strikes at the university, where they occupied the buildings, sleeping on tables. The shops were empty and the atmosphere was tense. But the days described here were leading up to the inevitable crisis that came on 13 December 1981, when martial law was imposed, General Jaruzelski was put in charge of the country, tanks rolled through the streets of the major cities, and many people were arrested.

Olga Tokarczuk has since enjoyed a highly successful career as a novelist and essayist, culminating in winning the 2018 Nobel Prize in Literature. Much of her work is set in the Kłodzko Valley in south-western Poland where she lives, but one of her most familiar short stories is 'Professor Andrews Goes to Warsaw', about a baffled foreign visitor who arrives in the city to give a lecture in December 1981, just after martial law is declared. Unable to speak a word of Polish, and mostly abandoned by the academics who have invited him, he has a confusing stay in the run-up to Christmas. The story was translated into English by Kim Jastremski and can be found on the Visegrad Group website.

Krzysztof Varga (b. 1968) Like the narrator of the first story in this collection, Patryk, the young hero of 'Return of the Evil One' (written exactly 100 years later by essayist, journalist, and novelist Krzysztof Varga), goes through a time warp, waking up almost sixty years in the past, in the Warsaw of 1955. But he has also gone through a literary portal, because the mysterious man who saves his life is instantly recognizable to Polish readers as the hero of one of the most famous novels set in Warsaw—*Zły* by Leopold Tyrmand, the title of which means 'The Evil One' (translated into English by David Welsh and published in 1958 by Michael Joseph as *Zly*, then in 1959 as *The Man with the White Eyes*), about a vigilante who fights the hooligans and petty criminals that are a blight on the city, and who has the tacit approval of the militia. Various characters and incidents from the novel are mentioned in Varga's story. The photograph illustrating the story is a portrait of 'The Man with the White Eyes', a genuine mural painted on the wall of the Deaf-and-Dumb Institute, which also features in this text.

This is a very recognizable part of central Warsaw, and once again in this story Warsaw's past encroaches on its present; as in 'Apparitions', the opening story of this collection, here we have a strange vision that transports the central character to a different era. Another contemporary author and lifelong resident of Warsaw is Zygmunt Miłoszewski, whose popular crime novels include the murder mystery *Entanglement*, featuring many identifiable locations within the city centre, and including scenes set in the same cafés that appear in Varga's story. *Entanglement* is available from Bitter Lemon Press (2010) in translation by Antonia Lloyd-Jones, and provides an entertaining alternative guide to the central part of the city.

Publisher's Acknowledgements

Maria Kuncewiczowa, 'ZOO', from *Dyliżans warszawski*, Instytut Wydawniczy 'PAX', Warsaw, 1958. 'ZOO' is reproduced by kind permission of the Kuncewicz Family House branch of the Vistula River Museum in Kazimierz Dolny. Copyright © Muzeum Nadwiślańskie w Kazimierzy Dolnym, Oddział Dom Kuncewiczów.

Jarosław Iwaszkiewicz, 'Ikar', from *Opowiadania zebrane*, Vol 2, Czytelnik, Warsaw 1960. 'Icarus' is reproduced by kind permission of the estate of Jarosław Iwaszkiewicz. Copyright © the estate of Jarosław Iwaszkiewicz.

Ludwik Hering, 'Ślady', from *Ślady, Opowiadania*, Wydawnictwo Czarna Owca, Warsaw 2017. 'Traces' is reproduced by kind permission of Ludmiła Murawska-Péju. Copyright © Ludmiła Murawska-Péju.

Zofia Petersowa, 'Pogrzeb', from *Odwet: Opowieści okupacyjne*, Księgarni, Łódź 1947. 'The Funeral' is reproduced by kind permission of the Związek Literatów Polskich (Polish Writers' Union). Copyright © Związek Literatów Polskich.

Marek Hłasko, 'Pierwszy krok w chmurach', from *Pierwszy krok w chmurach*, Agora SA, Warsaw, 2014. 'First Step in the Clouds' is reproduced by kind permission of Agnieszka Czyżewska. Copyright © Agnieszka Czyżewska.

Kazimierz Orłoś, 'Pałac Kultury', from *Powrót*, Wydawnictwo Literackie, Kraków 2021. 'The Palace of Culture' is reproduced by kind permission of the author. Copyright © Kazimierz Orłoś.

Hanna Krall, 'Obecność' from *Fantom bólu: Wszystkie reportaże*, Wydawnictwo Literackie, Kraków 2017. 'The Presence' is reproduced by kind permission of the author. Copyright © Hanna Krall.

Antoni Libera, 'Widok z góry i z dołu', from *Niech się panu darzy i dwie inne nowele*, Biblioteka 'WIĘZI', Warsaw 2013. 'The View from Above and Below' is reproduced by kind permission of the author. Copyright © Antoni Libera.

Zbigniew Mentzel, 'Mapa Warszawy', from *Niebezpieczne narzędzie w ustach*, słowo/obraz terytoria, Gdańsk 2001. 'The Warsaw Map' is reproduced by kind permission of the author. Copyright © Zbigniew Mentzel.

Olga Tokarczuk, 'Che Guevara', from *Gra na wielu bębenkach*, Wydawnictwo Ruta, Wałbrzych 2001. 'Che Guevara' is reproduced by kind permission of the author, c/o Rogers Coleridge & White Ltd, 20 Powis Mews, London W11 1JN. Copyright © Olga Tokarczuk.

Krzysztof Varga, 'Powrót Złego', in *Mówi Warszawa*, Muzeum Powstania Warszawskiego, Instytut Stefana Starzyńskiego, and Wydawnictwo Trio, Warsaw 2011. 'Return of the Evil One' is reproduced by kind permission of the author. Copyright © Krzysztof Varga.

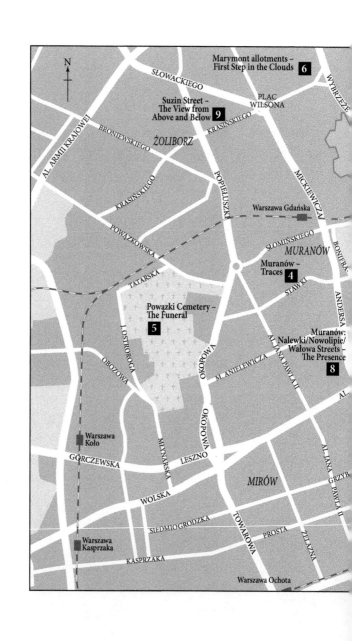

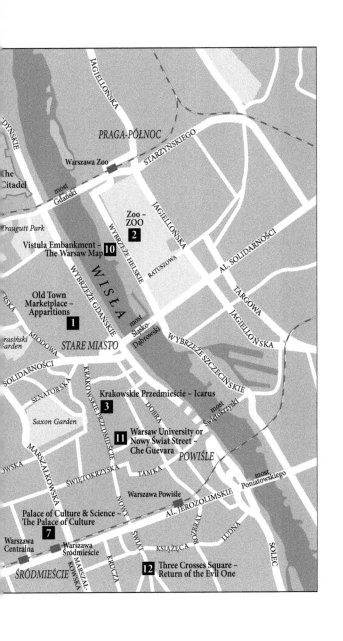

PRAGA-PÓŁNOC

JAGIELLOŃSKA

STARZYNSKIEGO

Warszawa Zoo

The
Citadel

most
Gdański

Traugutt Park

Zoo –
ZOO
2

JAGIELLOŃSKA

WYBRZEŻE HELSKIE

RATUSZOWA

AL. SOLIDARNOŚCI

Vistula Embankment –
The Warsaw Map **10**

W I S Ł A

Old Town
Marketplace –
Apparitions
1

WYBRZEŻE GDAŃSKIE

TARGOWA

JAGIELLOŃSKA

rasiński
arden

MIODOWA

STARE MIASTO

most
Śląsko-
Dąbrowski

WYBRZEŻE SZCZECIŃSKIE

SOLIDARNOŚCI

SENATORSKA

KRAKOWSKIE PRZEDMIEŚCIE

Krakowskie Przedmieście – Icarus
3

DOBRA

most
Świętokrzyski

Saxon Garden

Warsaw University or
Nowy Świat Street –
Che Guevara **11**

POWIŚLE

MARSZAŁKOWSKA

OWSKA

ŚWIĘTOKRZYSKA

TAMKA

most
Poniatowskiego

Warszawa Powiśle

NOWY

AL. JEROZOLIMSKIE

Palace of Culture & Science –
The Palace of Culture
7

ŚWIAT

ROZBRAT

LUDNA

SOLEC

Warszawa
Centralna

Warszawa
Śródmieście

KSIĄŻĘCA

MARSZAŁ-
KOWSKA

KRUCZA

Three Crosses Square –
Return of the Evil One **12**

ŚRÓDMIEŚCIE